THE CUBAN GAMBIT

ALSO BY BRENT TOWNS

Team Reaper Thrillers

Fear the Reaper Series

The MI6 Files

Talon Series

Mark Hayes Series

Dave Nash Thrillers

Treasure Series

The Gods of War Series

Genocide

Congo Ice

Stalin's Spear

THE CUBAN GAMBIT

THE GODS OF WAR
BOOK 4

BRENT TOWNS

ROUGH
EDGES
PRESS

The Cuban Gambit
Paperback Edition
Copyright © 2024 Brent Towns

Rough Edges Press
An Imprint of Wolfpack Publishing
1707 E. Diana Street
Tampa, FL 33610

roughedgespress.com

Paperback ISBN 978-1-68549-363-9
eBook ISBN 978-1-68549-362-2
LCCN 2024943185

THE CUBAN GAMBIT

MI6 INTERROGATION SITE, LONDON

I WAS BACK, AND THIS TIME, I WAS ALONE. INTERROGATION, DAY 4. Lined up across the other side of the table were four seats. The people I was waiting for. You all know me by now. John **Reaper** Kane. I was part of a taskforce that started investigating an incident in Syria, which quickly spiraled out of control.

Since then, we'd been fighting every step of the way against a force known as the Gods of War. Mind you, their numbers were less now than when we had begun. But that didn't stop them. Not Mikhail Shatov. He was bound to see it through to the very end.

Today was my day. Mine, with no moral support from my teammate Ray Knocker Jensen. You see, the team at this point in the debrief had been separated, not requiring the others for the moment. Which was fine by me because they were busy with a special prisoner.

In the doorway there was a subtle shift as my interrogators entered, led by Christine Ryan. Her short dark hair framed sharp, eagle-like eyes, and her athletic build exuded confidence. Today, she wore a dark skirt that harmonized with her hair and lipstick, paired with a crisp white cotton blouse. Her companions, Charles German, Jack Holland, and Ken Newman, all donned suits. Their once-vibrant hair now showed traces of gray, marking their forties. Among them, Ken Newman held the position of the current CIA director.

My hair was dark, and I hadn't shaved for a week, so I was sporting a short dark beard across my jaw. The moniker Reaper was derived from the tattoo on my back.

"Mr. Kane," Christine Ryan said by way of greeting.

"Ma'am."

The other three individuals regarded me with a mixture of disdain and indifference. Each of them brandished a folder, swiftly flipping it open to extract specific documents, which they then arranged neatly before themselves.

Christine Ryan stared at me. It was obvious that she had paid extra attention to her appearance this morning, her makeup expertly applied, seeming to take about ten years off her age. "Mr. Kane, when we wrapped-up yesterday, you had just received news about South Korea. Correct?"

"Yes, ma'am."

"You also ascertained that Sergey Lash was the person in overall command of the operation, yes?"

"That's what we thought, ma'am. At the time."

Opening her mouth to speak again, she was distracted by a movement at the door. Turning my head to investigate the interruption, I grinned broadly as Holly Smith and Knocker entered the room.

German said, "I thought you were told your presence wasn't required today."

Holly nodded. "We were, but decided to come anyway."

The late arrivals selected chairs and sat down, looking up as Christine Ryan said, "So, shall we start with the operation in South Korea?"

"No, ma'am."

"No?" She seemed surprised.

"This time, it started with a new crisis in Cuba."

THE CUBAN CRISIS

THE ANTONOV AN-25 AIRCRAFT DESCENDED GRACEFULLY, ITS tires leaving black marks on the concrete runway. A puff of smoke rose as it touched down, and the giant beast's nose dipped, mimicked by the twin set of nose wheels. The six turbines roared to life as the pilot engaged reverse thrust, gradually slowing the monster until it reached taxiing speed.

The aircraft lumbered along the runway, retracing its path from the recent landing. It then turned once more, heading toward the apron where it would come to a stop for unloading.

Two men observed as it rolled to a halt. One wore the crisp uniform of a Cuban military officer, while the other donned casual attire, complete with a vibrant floral Hawaiian shirt. The latter man chewed on a hefty cigar wedged into the corner of his mouth.

"This is a big responsibility for you, Julio," the military officer said to the man beside him.

"The greater the responsibility, the bigger the payday, Pedro," replied the drug cartel boss Julio Garcia.

"This is bigger than your drug empire," Pedro Martinez pointed out. "Much, much bigger. This could bring the might of the United States down upon us."

"That is why the missiles need to be kept hidden away,"

Garcia replied. "In their present condition, they are useless. Once these engines are in place and the microchips are installed, then it will be a different story."

"For who, Julio? The missiles are in our yard. In Cuba, not in Russia."

"You worry too much, Pedro. All will be good once it starts."

"And what of the mercenary team the Russians are worried about?" Martinez asked.

"Do you not support this move, Pedro?" Garcia asked suspiciously.

"I will back you, Julio, but I want it known that I do not support this move at all. This will bring Cuba nothing but trouble."

"Once again, I thank you, Pedro," Garcia said to his friend.

"For what?"

"Your honesty," Garcia replied, drawing a gold-plated .44 Magnum from his belt and shooting his friend in the head.

Moving the cigar from one side of his mouth to the other, Garcia deftly returned the handgun to its concealed position in his pants. Standing there, he observed with keen interest as five pristine rocket motors were carefully unloaded from the Antonov cargo plane and placed onto five waiting trucks.

With the loading complete, the trucks started to move off, exiting through the gates of the fenced-off area and away from the airfield. Each with its own secret destination, the drivers were privy only to their own route.

As the final vehicle vanished into the distance, Julio Garcia plucked the cigar from between his teeth and broke into a wide grin. This day was shaping up to be extraordinary. Soon, Cuba would rise once more as a formidable nation, and it would owe its resurgence to none other than Julio Garcia.

President Julio Garcia. It had a certain ring to it.

CHAPTER 1

IN SEOUL, SOUTH KOREA, I FOUND MYSELF ON ANOTHER COVERT mission, guided by intelligence from an old friend. The city hummed with life, its neon-lit alleys concealing secrets and shadows.

I was here after Gennady Morozov, a man I had sworn to bring in or kill. He was one of the enigmatic generals known as the Gods of War, men who wielded power beyond borders. His presence alone meant trouble.

But Morozov was not alone. The scientist, Sepp Kahn, was with him, their alliance bound by a shared purpose.

The team's deduction led us to a singular conclusion. They sought microchips—tiny, potent fragments of technology. These were no ordinary chips. They were the missing link, spanning the gap between past and future. Their purpose? To breathe new life into the aging R-12 ballistic missiles, weapons of a bygone era, relics of Cold War tensions.

I took a cab from the Incheon International Airport to the Seoul Ramada hotel. It was a large resort-style affair that catered to the wealthy and the famous. Of which I was neither, but when MI6 is paying the bill, why not?

After completing the check-in process, I took the elevator and then walked the corridor to my assigned room, my bag in tow. Upon entering, I dropped it onto the bed and then made my way to the double glass sliding doors. As I pushed them open, I stepped out onto the balcony. From this vantage point on the sixth floor, I looked downward. Below me stretched a spacious pool encircled by lush gardens and winding paths. Neatly arranged sun lounges adorned the expansive paved area, inviting relaxation and leisure. Despite the cooler weather, most of the lounges were already occupied.

Re-entering the room, I walked over to check out the minibar refrigerator. Bending down, I saw two beers and several sodas in the door, so I took a beer and cracked the top off it. The beer was cold and tasted fine, so I took another pull. The buzzing of my cell drew my attention, and I picked it up, looking at the screen. Pressing the answer key, I said, "Jones."

That was the name I had checked in under. Sam Jones. According to my passport, I was an engineer in Seoul for a conference on new building materials.

"Hello, Mr. Jones." It was Holly.

"Boss."

"Are you settling in okay?"

"Yes, fine. You should see this place."

"I'm happy you like it. Just don't run up the tab too high."

I looked down at the beer in my hand, then shrugged. "Are you calling me for a reason?"

"When you are finished in Seoul, I need you to go to Cuba. Our agent there has provided some solid intel. I'll give you the condensed version of what we have. Once you arrive, you'll receive new orders, John."

"Yes, ma'am."

"Okay, good luck."

Disconnecting the call, I considered the upcoming mission, which filled me with a sense of unease. Moments later, my phone buzzed, alerting me to the arrival of a new message. When I opened it, I was faced with a series of images on my screen, each one vying for my attention.

The first photo depicted the Antonov, its massive form dominating the frame. Trucks parked, men unloading cargo from its cavernous hold. The sheer scale of the aircraft was awe-inspiring. Next came closer shots of the rocket engines.

Then, the focus shifted to two men. Strangers to me, their faces unfamiliar. Who were they? What role did they play, and where did they fit in this whole puzzle? I knew answers would come, but for now, they remained elusive.

And finally, the image that stopped me cold. The man in the Hawaiian shirt, in his hand a gold handgun that gleamed malevolently. The military officer lay crumpled at his feet, blood pooling around him. The stark contrast between aloha prints and violence was jarring.

Questions swirled in my mind as I tried to make sense of what had happened. I guess I would find out eventually, but until then, I had another mission to concentrate on.

Suddenly overwhelmed by an all-encompassing sense of fatigue, I flopped back on the bed, closing my eyes, letting the jetlag wash over me. When I awoke, it was dark.

The luminescent hands of my watch informed me that it was early evening, so I rubbed my eyes, deciding to shower and head to the restaurant for a meal and something to drink.

———

Perched high above on the rooftop, the Moonlit Terrace was a haven looking out over the bustling streets of Seoul.

The entrance was discreet, tucked away behind a velvet curtain adorned with silver embroidery. As guests exited the elevator, they were greeted by the soft strains of a jazz singer. It was dimly lit, creating a soft ambiance. Lanterns hung from twisted hooks, casting dappled shadows on the polished wooden floor.

Tables, draped in midnight-blue linens, stood along a

steel balustrade. Each held a single rose, its petals soft and moist. Patrons leaned in, talking softly. The scent of jasmine and roasted chestnuts hung in the air, a fragrant dance that teased the senses, making me hungry.

I sat at a table and picked up a menu. It was a balance of Korean flavors and international flair.

The hostess flitted among the tables, smiling at patrons and taking drink orders. When she finally reached mine, her soft voice greeted me: "Good evening, sir. Would you like to order or maybe a glass of wine?"

I stared into her dark eyes, made even more so by the ring of kohl applied expertly to accentuate them. Her smile was broad, her teeth white, yet her frame was thin and her features fine. "Maybe a beer?"

Her smile remained. "One beer coming up. Any preference?"

I shook my head. "Surprise me."

By the time she returned with my drink, I had perused the menu, deciding on the Bulgogi. I grinned at the hostess. "I hope I said that right?"

Once again, she smiled at me. "Even if you didn't, I would never correct you. In my culture, it would be considered rude."

Looking out across the sparkling city, I drank my beer while awaiting my food. The dish arrived, and I found it quite delightful. Despite being a first-time experience, I would gladly indulge in it again if given the opportunity.

I was almost done when two men entered the restaurant. They were tall and solidly built. Not quite up to my six-four, but close. They carried themselves in a manner that bespoke extensive military training.

Their presence set my senses on heightened alert, and my eyes darted around the restaurant, picking out two more. A man and woman. This wasn't the place to be locked in battle with four killers—if that's what they were.

Finishing my meal, I drank the last of my beer and wiped my mouth on the napkin, standing up to leave. Using sleight of hand, I requisitioned the knife from the table, having come without a handgun.

Moving through the tables toward the elevator, I pressed the call button and waited. Moments later, I was joined by the two men. With a soft chime, the elevator car arrived, and we stepped into its hushed depths. The muted tones of its interior were warm and inviting. Glancing around surreptitiously, I noticed a camera situated in the top right corner of the car.

My side throbbed as the cold steel of a handgun pressed against it. A heavily accented voice, close to my ear, delivered a chilling ultimatum. "Do not move or I will kill you, Mr. Kane."

"I'm afraid you have me at a disadvantage," I replied. "You know mine, so I guess that makes us friends."

"Unlikely," the man grunted.

"Where to now?" I asked.

"Somewhere nice and quiet."

"It'll have to be," I said. "Too many cameras otherwise."

They led me down to the foyer and out through the front doors. However, they made a critical oversight, failing to check me thoroughly for weapons. I was put in the back of an SUV, where we were joined by the other two individuals. The woman settled into the front passenger seat while two men took their places beside me in the back.

The alley they guided me to lay hidden in the heart of Seoul, far removed from the bustling streets and neon lights. Within its narrow confines, shadows clung to the walls like stubborn glue. As we drove deeper into its depths, the sounds of the city faded to a distant hum.

The pavement beneath our tires bore the scars of countless vehicles, its surface uneven from years of wear and tear. Graffiti adorned the walls on either side. Some of the vibrant murals seemed to tell stories, while other tags were mere junk, hastily sprayed by talentless kids with idle hands.

As our SUV rolled to a stop, a stray cat emerged from the shadows. Its fur was matted, and its eyes glinted like demonic orbs, reflecting the harsh headlamp beams. For a moment, it seemed possessed, its plaintive squeal echoing through the night.

Next to me, one of the men attached a suppressor to the handgun he was holding before swinging open the door. "Get out," he commanded.

I thought about the knife I had pilfered from the table, recalling the old adage about bringing a knife to a gunfight. Unfortunately, it was all I had. Someone was going to die, and I was determined it wasn't going to be me.

The blade swept in a deadly arc, plunging deep into the killer's throat. With a swift, slicing motion, I yanked it out, severing everything it touched. Blood sprayed across the vehicle's interior, creating a gruesome pattern on the seats and windows.

Summoning all my strength, I swung the blood-soaked blade back around, aiming for the man on my opposite side. His hand shot up in a desperate attempt to shield himself, but the blade pierced through it, eliciting a sharp yelp of pain.

Bringing my elbow up, I hit him in the face. His cries of pain stopped as his head snapped back, rendering him unconscious. I reached down and grabbed the suppressed handgun, hoping that it was ready to fire.

Pointing it at the back of the driver's head, I squeezed the trigger, sending a shower of blood and brain matter across the dash and front window. Which left only the woman in the front passenger seat. I had the gun trained on her, and her face was a mask of fear as she sat frozen, unable to move.

"Who sent you?"

She said nothing.

I pushed the suppressor against her head forcefully. "I won't ask again."

"Grigori."

"Who is Grigori?"

"Grigori Igoshin."

She spoke the words as though they should mean something to me, but even after racking my brain, I couldn't come up with anything with that handle. "Who is he?"

"The one who will kill you for what you have done," she hissed.

"Do you have a gun?"

She remained silent, but her cool blue eyes gave her away. I reached out. "Give it to me."

After a brief hesitation, the handgun was passed over, and I dismantled it. "Get out."

"What?"

"Get out and start walking."

"You are letting me go?" Her tone was incredulous.

"It's either that or kill you, and I think there has already been enough of that."

The woman looked hesitantly at me, making sure I wasn't lying, before reaching to open the door. She climbed out and then started walking away before increasing her pace to a fast jog. Moments later, soaked in blood, I slipped out of the vehicle. Watching the woman until she disappeared, I then headed back toward the hotel, using the same vehicle to get me close enough to walk the rest of the way.

———

Making it to the hotel unmolested by further assailants, I slipped stealthily into the hotel through the rear entrance. The warm water cascaded over me as I stood beneath the shower, washing away the remnants of dried blood. My blood-stained clothes were hastily bundled into a plastic bag and tossed unceremoniously down the trash chute. The late hour weighed heavily on my weary body, urging me toward the comfort of the bed. Tonight, I was to rendezvous with my friend from Czech intelligence—or so I thought.

The knock on the door put me on edge. "Who is it?"

"It is me."

I recognized the voice immediately. Hastily, I crossed the room and swung open the door. The gray-haired man, clad in a long coat and suit, slipped inside, and I shut the door behind him. He turned toward me, extending his hand. "It is good to see you, John," he said.

"You too, Jan," I replied, taking his hand.

Jan Koller was the man I was here to meet. A veteran of Czech intelligence, he'd been a shadow throughout Europe for what seemed a lifetime.

"You look on edge, my friend," Koller said.

"I had a welcoming committee," I informed him. "Mercenaries from someone named Grigori Igoshin."

He shook his head solemnly. "Oh, my, you have hit it big already."

"Who is he?"

"Like you said, he is a mercenary. A nasty man who sells his soul to the oligarchs in Russia. Last year, he and his people wiped out a village in Kazakhstan. It was sitting on an oil field."

"Another one," I muttered.

"What do you mean?" Koller asked with a frown.

I told him about the village in Syria.

"You let the woman go?" he asked.

I nodded. "Yes."

"Then it is a good thing I brought you this."

Koller reached into his coat pocket and withdrew a Glock, along with some ammunition and a spare magazine.

"Thank you, Jan. Now, tell me about this meeting. More to the point, how do you know about Morozov?"

He gave me a tentative smile. "We go back a long way, Gennady and myself. Remember, I am not a young man. I will not bore you with the details. But one day, he resurfaced. We were investigating the deaths of some old East German agents. It was unusual because we were Czech. But one of them was a friend of mine. That is how I found out about Gennady. Then I heard you were looking for him, and he surfaced in Prague with Sepp Kahn. Why are you after them?"

"Stalin's Spear," I replied.

Koller nodded slowly. "There is a name I have not heard in a long time. I first came across it when I was digging through some old intelligence files. Initially, when I heard of it, I thought it was a myth. But the files told me otherwise."

"Ever heard of Mikhail Shatov?" I asked.

"Another old name."

"Okay, before I go on, just one more. The Gods of War."

Koller chuckled. "That one I know is a myth. A tale that made the rounds of KGB circles back in the day by old intelligence warriors."

I shook my head. "Sorry, Jan, it's about as real as it gets. I think there are five—were five of them, including Shatov and Morozov."

"Were?"

"We've killed two of them. Well, we killed one, and Shatov killed another of his own to ensure we couldn't get to him."

"Oh, dear, you'd better tell it all to me, John."

I spent the next ten minutes giving him a rundown of what I knew. Even the operation onto Wrangel Island. Once I was done, the look on my friend's face told me he was astounded by what he'd heard.

"Stop there, Mr. Kane," German said. "Am I to understand that you shared classified intelligence with a foreign agent?"

"We share intel with other agencies all the time," I pointed out.

"Yes, but not anything like this, and with a former communist state to boot? Even you just said that your friend worked with the KGB and East German police."

"I would trust that man with my life," I replied. "He is a lot more honest than some people I know."

"What is that supposed to mean?"

"Whatever."

I stared at Koller. "We think Morozov and the scientist are here buying more microchips for the motors they're going to put in the R-12s. The last ones were being transported by plane when it crashed."

"That would make it so. They had a meeting with an

electronic specialist yesterday. We could maybe go and pay him a visit."

"What is his name?" I asked.

"Jae-sung Lee," Koller told me. "He works either side of the law. Which is how he made his fortune. Some intel has him also supplying the North Koreans."

"Sounds like someone I need to talk to," Kane said.

"I will come by tomorrow and we will go together," Koller said to me.

I shook my head. "No, Jan. You have done enough."

"Are you shutting me out, John?" he asked, looking a little put out.

"Yes, Jan, I am. These people are killers. I've already lost more than one friend in this, and a lot of innocents have died along the way. Go back to Prague, Jan. Get as far away from this as possible."

"If I didn't know you, John, I would be very angry with what I would class as disrespect. But I do know you, and I also know that you are coming from a place of deep concern. So, I will do as you say and return to Prague."

"Thank you, Jan. For everything."

CHAPTER 2

THE NEXT MORNING FOUND ME WIDE AWAKE AND BRACED FOR whatever challenges lay ahead. However, the unexpected arrival of Yu-mi Kim caught me off-guard. Just as I had stepped out of the shower, a sharp rap on my door shattered the tranquility of the morning. Hastily wrapping myself in a towel, I answered the door, unprepared for the encounter that awaited me.

Kim stood before me, her presence commanding attention with her fine features framed by long, dark locks cascading over her shoulders. Her slender figure held an air of grace and confidence, her stature nearly matching my own. Clad in a sleek dark suit, she exuded an aura of authority that left little room for doubt.

"Who are you?" I queried, my tone clipped with a hint of skepticism as I struggled to reconcile her unexpected appearance with the plans I had meticulously laid out.

"I am Yu-mi Kim," she responded evenly, her voice carrying a hint of intrigue as she stepped into my room. "You can call me Kim."

"What are you doing here?" I asked her.

Her eyes ran across my chest, taking in the terrain of my scars. "Maybe you should get dressed first and then I will tell you."

I went into the bedroom and hastily pulled clothes on, starting with jeans. Once dressed and armed, I came out to find Kim seated on the sofa. "Have a seat, Mr. Kane—"

"John," I corrected her.

"John."

"Or Reaper."

"Reaper? How savage."

I nodded. "I've been accused of that more than a few times in life. Now, back to you."

"I work for NIS," Kim said to me.

I was confused for a moment. "Why is Korean Intelligence interested in me?"

"It would seem we have a mutual friend," she replied.

"Jan Koller?"

"Yes. He asked that I keep an eye on you just in case you became mired in something that you couldn't handle alone."

"Did he mention who I was after?"

"He said it was dangerous."

"Yet you are here," I said.

"It couldn't be any worse than operating in the north for weeks on end," Kim replied.

She had me there. "All right, it'll be good to have someone who knows their way around."

"Just so you know, I will not sleep with you."

I frowned. "Why would you even say that?"

"I like to be upfront about things. Besides, you seem to be someone who might try something like that."

With a half smile, I said, "You should meet my friend."

"I do not think so. What is your plan?"

"To go and see Jae-sung Lee," I told her.

"You mean Lee Jae-sung. We say the surname first here in South Korea."

"How about I just call him Lee and be done with it?"

"Fine. Why are you going to see him?"

"Because he's the man with the technology," I replied. "Which—"

A knock at the door stopped me. I gave Kim a warning glance and pressed a finger to my lips. "Who is it?"

"Room service with your breakfast."

My gaze lingered on Kim for a moment, processing the unexpected turn of events before a flicker of realization prompted me to gesture toward the breakfast trolley left in the corner of the room. With a silent nod of understanding, Kim swiftly moved to conceal the trolley from view, her movements deft and purposeful as she navigated the space with ease.

As she silently obscured the telltale sign, I watched as a sleek handgun materialized in her hands, accompanied by the addition of a suppressor. Without hesitation, she expertly affixed the suppressor to the weapon.

"Be right there," I replied.

Opening the door, I stepped back and let the man in with the trolley. "Morning, sir."

"Morning, take it on in."

He wheeled it into the center of the room, where he spotted Kim. He nodded at her. "Ma'am."

"Just leave it there," I said to him.

"Yes, sir."

He certainly possessed a swift reflex, I'd give him that much, yet it proved insufficient in the end. With a practiced motion, he raised his suppressed handgun, swiftly pivoting toward me, under the impression that I posed the primary threat to his mission's success. However, his assessment was flawed. In his final moments, he clung to the mistaken belief that I was his adversary, sealing his fate.

Meanwhile, Kim, with her own firearm at the ready, unleashed a decisive shot that tore through the side of his head. His body crumpled sideways. The firearm he'd intended to deploy remained untouched. Looking on, I groaned, "I had hoped to glean some information from him."

Kim offered a nonchalant shrug in response. "Sorry," she

muttered, displaying little remorse for the missed opportunity.

I bent down and checked him over. There was no doubt he was dead, and I couldn't find anything identifying him. It made me wonder whether he was one of Grigori's or Morozov's men.

Meanwhile, Kim was on a call. When she was finished, she said, "Someone will be here shortly to tidy this up. In the meantime, grab your things and I'll take you somewhere a little safer."

——

Five minutes after throwing my things together, we were navigating the bustling streets of Seoul within the confines of a compact Hyundai. Materializing before us was our destination, a towering apartment block looming above the urban landscape. Ascending swiftly via the elevator, we got out on the sixth floor and walked the length of a corridor, arriving at a modest two-bedroom apartment.

Crossing the threshold, we were greeted by a feline resident, a black and white furball with an excessive amount of affection. Kim scooped up the creature, and I trailed behind her as we ventured further into the apartment. "What is this place?" I inquired, scanning the unfamiliar surroundings.

"It's my home," she responded matter-of-factly, extending a hospitable gesture. "Allow me to relieve you of your bag."

I handed it over, and while she was gone, my gaze was drawn to a picture on a shelf. It was of a young woman in uniform wearing a beret. "That seems like a lifetime ago," Kim said as she reappeared.

"How long did you serve?"

"Six years before I was recruited into intelligence," she replied.

"Did you see any combat?"

"Afghanistan for a few months."

I nodded. "What is the cat's name?"

Kim told me, but I didn't understand. It must have been obvious because then she said, "Lazy."

"That I understand."

"Shall we go and see Lee now?" Kim asked.

"I don't see why not."

———

After swapping her Hyundai for an armored-up Genesis GV80, she headed for Lee's place of business. From behind the wheel, Kim smiled at me and said, "Just in case."

The journey took us to a sprawling complex, somewhat like an expansive industrial park. The structures towered over us, interconnected by miles of concrete drives.

"Quite imposing," I remarked to Kim as we surveyed the vast premises.

"It certainly is," she affirmed, her tone reflecting a familiarity with the surroundings.

Parking our vehicle amid the sea of asphalt, we ventured inside. The lobby greeted us with an air of opulence that contrasted sharply with the industrial exterior. The small reception desk seemed almost intimate, inconsequential against the backdrop of the colossal marble floor that stretched endlessly.

Approaching the receptionist, Kim announced our intention to see Lee. With a polite nod, the woman requested a moment to make a call. Following a brief exchange, she turned back to us with an apologetic expression. "Mr. Lee is currently occupied. You'll need to reschedule your visit."

Kim took out her identification and said, "Call him again."

"But—"

"Do it."

The woman made the call, and after a few more moments, she hung up and said, "Take the elevator to the top floor. Mr. Lee is waiting for you."

As we crossed to the bank of gleaming elevators, Kim pressed the button, and we waited for it to arrive. When the doors slid open, we found ourselves staring down the barrel of three guns, each with a large man holding it. I glanced at Kim and said, "Someone isn't happy to see us."

The men relieved us of our weapons and ushered us into the elevator car. I said to the guy who'd taken my gun, "I'll be having that back when I leave."

He grunted by way of response but said no more. Once at the top floor, the doors slid open, and we stepped out onto a luxuriously thick carpet that seemed to extend for miles, the large suite having been converted into an office.

Lee wasn't a big man, but he did have an imposing presence about him. He stood in the middle of his suite and greeted us. "Good morning. Ms. Kim, I have met before, but you, Mr. Kane, I have only heard about."

I glanced at Kim. "You know him?"

"Yes."

"You didn't think to mention that?"

"He's not worth mentioning."

"Is that any way to speak about your brother?" he asked.

My eyebrows shot up. "Your brother?"

"It is a long story."

Lee smiled. His eyes locked on me. "I know what I have to do with you, but what shall I do with my sister?"

"You could return her gun and wave her goodbye," I suggested.

"I could, but she is more likely to shoot me than to wave back."

"You are an asshole, Jae-sung," Lee hissed. "Working with the Russians."

"And you are so altruistic yourself? It is business. That is all."

"So, what now? You kill me here and dump the body? I don't see any plastic on the floor."

"You watch too many movies, my American friend. My men will take you outside the city and kill you there. They will bury you in a deep hole and bring back something to prove that they have accomplished their mission. As for my sister, in a couple of days, after my business is complete, I will let her go."

I glanced at Kim. She seemed deceptively calm and cool, considering the circumstances. I said, "I'll be back for you. Then you can kill him."

"Don't take too long," she replied coldly. "Sometimes I can become very impatient."

"Take him away," Lee snapped.

As I was escorted back toward the elevator, I said to the guy on my left, "Did you bring my gun?"

He opened his jacket, showing it tucked snugly into his waistband.

Nodding, I said, "Good, I'd hate to have made you go back to get it."

The elevator took us down into a subterranean garage. Before putting me into the rear of an SUV, one of my newly acquired friends zippy-tied my hands behind my back. I wasn't worried too much about this. Being a strong man with powerful arms, I figured I could get out of them without any problem.

We traversed the streets of Seoul until reaching the outskirts of the city. The driver continued for a while and then turned off onto a secondary road, which took us into a thick forest. He pulled off the road and into a large turnout.

The guy who had my gun helped me out of the rear seat by dragging me clear. Both men escorted me away from the vehicle along a narrow track. The rich and musty smell of damp earth and decomposing leaves grew more intense the further we went.

After ten minutes of walking, my friend said, "That is far enough."

I stopped and gazed up at the trees looming over us, drawing in a lung full of the forest's air. The birds were chirping, and I wondered if this was what others experienced before their imminent execution or just me as I calmly worked through the situation at hand.

"Get on your knees."

Like any good victim, I did as I was ordered and dropped down onto my knees. My friend kept me steady with a hand on my shoulder and then made his first and only mistake. He stepped in front of me, placing himself between me and the second man whose gun was trained on me.

This was my chance, and I made the most of it.

The muscles in my shoulders bunched, as did those in my arms. Using all the strength I could bring to bear, I forced my hands apart. The plastic gave way, and I was suddenly free. Bringing my left hand up, I grabbed the shirt of my new friend while my right went for the gun in his waistband.

His face was a mask of horror, pleading with his friend to intervene, and he knew in that moment that he was about to die.

"Told you I'd get it back."

Having removed the suppressor from the barrel before placing it in his waistband, the man had inadvertently made the weapon easier for me to handle. Ramming the muzzle deep into his stomach, I pulled the trigger twice. The man hunched under the hammer blows. I pushed him away and fired a third round into his head.

His friend was stunned to immobility as he stared at his dead partner. It gave me the edge I needed, and I fired the Glock in my hand twice, and he died too.

Checking their pockets, I found my cell. The other personal effects they'd taken from me were still in the SUV. No doubt they had planned to get rid of them later. I dragged the two bodies into the undergrowth and started back to the SUV. I needed to get to Lee before anything happened to Kim.

When I walked into the building, no one was more surprised to see me than the receptionist. Her jaw dropped, and she stammered, "S-sir, you can't be in here."

I smiled mirthlessly. "It's all right. Me and your boss are friends."

"Sir, I will call security."

"Maybe you should call the police," I replied, taking out the Glock as I headed toward the elevators.

A security guard stepped into view, an MP5 in his hands. My Glock fired before he could do the same, and he collapsed to the hard floor with a bullet in his leg. As blood pooled around him, I kicked his weapon away and grabbed his hand. "You might want to keep some pressure on that."

Then I summoned the elevator and climbed in.

When it reached the top, the doors opened, and a hailstorm of bullets hammered into it. Had I been inside, I would surely have died. But I was on top of the car and when it stopped, I dropped down and opened fire myself.

There were two shooters. Like the guard downstairs, both were armed with MP5s. I shot the first guy in the chest. Red stains began to flow from two holes in his white shirt. I shifted my aim and shot the next guy too. He died like his friend.

When I exited the elevator, I shot them both again, making sure that while I had my back to them, they weren't going to be an issue.

I saw Lee, pale-faced and scared, behind his desk. Kim sat on a sofa against a large floor-to-ceiling window, a guard with a handgun pointed at her head. Calmly, I said, "You shoot her, I'm going to shoot your boss. Then I'm going to shoot you."

He glanced at Lee, who rattled off something in Korean. The guard's stance changed, and he looked even more determined.

"I wouldn't," I reiterated.

Once more, he became uncertain and glanced at his boss for confirmation.

And I shot him.

The Glock discharging in the suite sounded like a cannon going off. I saw Kim flinch and then the guard fell to the floor with a hole in the side of his head, his brains splattered across the window.

The Glock came around and centered on Lee. "Right, motherfucker, it's time we had a chat."

CHAPTER 3

"Are you okay, Yu-mi?" I asked her as I stalked toward her brother.

"I am fine. What took you so long?"

"I was kind of tied up," I replied. "Keep an eye out the window, just in case the police come."

"It won't be the police," she informed me. "It'll be his hired thugs. Jae-sung has his own merry little army of hired killers."

"Then we'd better be quick," I said. "Where are the chips for Morozov?"

"Not here," he replied hurriedly.

I placed the muzzle of the gun against his leg. "I don't have time for this, Lee."

Panic crossed his face, and I caught him glancing at the far wall. I turned and looked. A painting. "You hiding a safe behind that thing?" I asked him.

"No."

The response was far too quick to be the truth. Crossing the room to the picture, I examined it more closely. It was sat on a hinge. With a tug, it swung away from the wall to reveal a safe. I turned to face Lee. "Well, well. Old school, huh? Get your scrawny ass over here."

He never moved.

"Yu-mi."

Kim strode purposefully across the room, her gaze fixed on the desk where her brother was seated. With a swift movement, she reached for the top drawer, its contents concealed until this moment. From within, she retrieved her weapon, its familiar weight reassuring in her hand.

Turning to face her brother, she found him startled by her sudden approach. Without a word, she seized him by the collar, her grip firm yet resolute. With a mixture of urgency and determination, she pulled him upright, his resistance feeble against her confidence.

"Come on, brother," she urged, her voice a low whisper that carried the weight of their shared history. "You're needed."

He protested all the way but eventually got there. I nodded. "Thanks, now you'd best go back to that window."

Grabbing Lee, I said, "Open it, or I'm going to start hurting you."

"I-I can't."

I hit him. Not very hard, but enough to sting and give him some encouragement. He yelped in surprise and backed away from me. I grabbed him before he got out of arm's reach and dragged him back. "Open the fucking safe."

"They're here, John," Kim called over to me.

Lee seemed to grow in confidence when he realized that time was now well and truly against us. But I wasn't done.

I grabbed the back of his head and rammed it into the wall beside the safe. "Open the fucking safe."

Blood ran from an abrasion on his forehead. He glared at me through the red mask and said, "You are a dead man, Mr. Kane. My men will find you and they will kill you. Nowhere in Seoul will be safe for you." He looked at Kim and spat vindictively: "The same for you, dear sister."

I hit him behind the ear with my Glock, dropping him like a stone. "Shit. Let's go, Yu-mi."

"Follow me. I know a back way out."

Within minutes, we were running across the parking lot to the SUV we'd arrived in. Climbing in, I asked her, "Where are we going?"

"Somewhere safe."

"We need to work out a way to get the chips before they are handed over to Morozov," I told her.

"We can't do that now, can we?" she said.

Thirty minutes later, the vehicle eased into the expansive driveway of a grand estate nestled amid lush gardens that seemed to stretch endlessly. At first glance, the house appeared unassuming, its elegant façade blending seamlessly with the surrounding landscape. Yet, as we drove the winding path toward the main entrance, my eyes caught glimpses of vigilant figures strategically stationed throughout the grounds, their presence conspicuous against the serene backdrop.

It came complete with armed guards, their stern expressions betraying the tranquility of the setting. "What is this place?"

Kim glanced at me briefly, a hint of gravity in her gaze before returning her attention to the road ahead. "Korean Intelligence safehouse with added security. We use it for only the most dangerous situations. Otherwise, I would take you back to my place."

"If I didn't know better, I would say you were flirting with me," I replied.

Her expression remained unchanged, so I let it go. My humor seemed to be wasted on her. Climbing from the SUV, we walked past two guards at the door before entering the house.

"How many guards here in total?" I asked Kim.

"Eight on each shift. Eight hours at a time."

She guided me through the tastefully decorated rooms of the mansion, each exuding an air of opulence befitting its upper-class status. To the casual observer, it could have easily passed for a luxurious residence, with its plush furnishings and tasteful décor. However, as we ventured deeper into the heart of the house, my eyes were drawn to a room unlike the others.

The security room stood in stark contrast to the elegance that filled the rest of the house. A multitude of screens adorned the walls, displaying live feeds from external cameras, their watchful gaze extending far beyond the confines of the estate. It was a testament to the vigilance that safeguarded the secrets harbored within these walls.

My gaze then fell upon the weapons cache, a sobering reminder of the reality that lurked beneath the facade of normalcy. Among the arsenal stood the KAC SR-16s, their presence commanding respect and underlining the seriousness of the defenses in place.

"Are all the guards former military?" I ventured, my curiosity piqued by the formidable array of weaponry.

Kim's response was solemn. "Yes," she confirmed, her voice carrying the weight of experience. "Black Berets," she added, the term resonating with an aura of respect and reverence reserved for those who had served in special forces.

I was about to say something when the guard monitoring the screens looked up and said, "The rest of the team is coming in."

I looked at the center screen and saw three SUVs entering through the main gate. "Who are they?" I asked Kim.

"My people. We need to get the chips from my brother, but failing that, we need to find your friend Morozov."

I found my respect growing. The meticulous organization of Kim's operation was awe-inspiring. As we stood in the driveway, sleek SUVs pulled up one by one, disgorging a diverse group of individuals, both women and men, each exuding an air of determination. With their arrival, the ranks swelled, adding an additional eight figures to our midst, seamlessly joining the existing team with practiced efficiency.

Observing their movements, it was evident that these newcomers were seasoned professionals, their every action methodical and deliberate as they wasted no time in getting down to business.

Kim's voice broke through the quiet anticipation that hung in the air, her words carrying a note of assurance amid the flurry of activity. "All we have to do now is wait," she remarked, her tone a blend of confidence and patience as she signaled for us to bide our time, trusting in the preparations that had been laid out.

———

It was just after dark when Kim's people came up with something we could use. She placed a picture in front of me.

"Min-Ho. South Korean mafia and a suspected Chinese agent. He specializes in drugs and prostitution. However, he has many safehouses throughout Seoul which are used to house certain guests." She placed another photo in front of me. "This happens to be one of them."

"That's him," I said.

"Yes, Gennady Morozov."

"Is this coming or going?" I asked.

"Coming. There is a good chance that he is still there."

"When do we leave?" I asked.

"Soon. We—"

Her words were interrupted by a large explosion from outside, then her earpiece lit up with incoming traffic. "What's happening?" I asked.

"We're being attacked," Kim said. "Quick, the security room."

We ran to the room and grabbed a couple of SR-16s. Along with spare ammo, we slipped on body armor. Back in the main security hub, the screens were going dark, one at a time. "How many of them?" Kim asked her man.

"Too many," he replied, coming to his feet. "You should leave, Yu-mi."

She reached out and touched his arm. "Take care."

"We are here for things like this."

He ran from the room, taking a weapon with him. I said, "What did he mean?"

"The security was put here to die so that people they guard may live. They are all volunteers."

"Brave men."

"Yes. Let's go."

Gunfire erupted from the front of the house. Kim grabbed my arm. "The back way."

She took point as I covered our rear. We sprinted toward the kitchen, adrenaline pumping. Just as we burst through the door, two shooters emerged from the shadows. Kim's SR-16 barked, and one of the assailants staggered backward. I pivoted to engage the second target, but Kim was already on it—her aim swift and deadly.

Two bursts of fire and two attackers were down.

Kim checked them with quiet efficiency, then muttered something I didn't quite catch. "You know them?"

"Min-Ho's men."

"The same Min-Ho you mentioned earlier?"

"Yes, he is a mercenary who also works for my brother," she replied.

She went out through the open door and onto a large, paved patio at the back. Kim covered right while I covered left. "We need to get around to our SUV."

A figure loomed up out of the darkness. I held my fire because I didn't know whether it was a bad guy or one of Kim's. However, as Kim turned, she fired immediately. "What is wrong with you?" she demanded.

"How can you tell which side they're on?"

"My people are better looking," she growled.

"What?"

"My people are all dead. I cannot raise them. It's just us. Any one you see, shoot."

I stood there, stunned by her revelation. How could she possibly know? Suddenly, another figure materialized out of the darkness. Without hesitation, I raised my weapon and fired. The figure staggered and fell, motionless where it lay.

"This way," Kim said.

I trailed behind Kim as we navigated through the sprawling expanse of the garden, its tranquility in stark contrast to the chaos unfolding around us. Water ponds dotted the landscape, their surfaces adorned with delicate lilies.

We pressed forward, drawn by the distant echoes of gunfire. More figures emerged from the shadows. With unwavering precision, Kim unleashed another fusillade of shots, her marksmanship undeniable as one of our adversaries crumpled to the ground.

Yet, before she could pivot to face the next threat, a sudden hail of gunfire erupted from across one of the ponds, the deafening barrage catching us off guard. Instinctively, we sought cover, the sound of bullets whizzing past serving as a chilling reminder of the stakes before us.

"Contact left!" I called out and started returning the incoming.

Firing at the muzzle flash because the shooter was in the shadows, I heard a yelp of pain and the shooting stopped. But the attack didn't. Two more adversaries rushed out of the darkness. I let the SR-16 fall and grabbed my Glock.

The first assailant closed in, almost upon me, when I squeezed the trigger. The Glock barked three times and the man crumpled to the ground. The second attacker slammed into me, jolting me sideways. Thankfully, my grip on the handgun remained firm. Rolling away, I regained my footing on one knee. The weapon bucked violently in my grasp, and the second assailant met his demise.

My senses heightened, adrenaline coursed through my veins as I scanned the surroundings for any lurking threats.

Amid the chaos, the unmistakable sounds of struggle broke through the clamor, drawing my attention like a magnet. There, during the fray, Kim found herself locked in a desperate tussle with yet another assailant.

Without hesitation, I closed the distance, my steps measured and purposeful as I approached the clash. With a steady hand, I pressed the muzzle of my weapon against the attacker's head, the cold metal a stark contrast against the heat of the moment. In one swift motion, I pulled the trigger, the deafening report of the gunshot echoing through the garden as the threat was neutralized.

As Kim rolled free from her attacker's grasp, I extended a hand to help her to her feet, relief flooding through me at the sight of her unharmed. "Are you okay?" I asked, my voice laced with concern, seeking reassurance in the wake of what we had just faced.

She nodded, a grateful smile tugging at the corners of her lips. "Yes, thanks," she replied, her tone reflecting her gratitude.

I picked up the SR-16 and said, "Let's go."

For the next five minutes, we moved in virtual silence as we weaved our way through the pathways of the garden while Min-Ho's men scoured the grounds in search of us. We took refuge behind a garden statue to survey the area where our vehicle was parked, looking for the slightest hint of danger.

In a silent exchange, I entrusted my SR-16 to Kim's capable hands, an unspoken acknowledgment of our shared trust and reliance on each other.

"Wait here," I murmured, my voice barely audible over the rustling leaves and distant shouts.

Maintaining a low profile, I used the dense foliage of the garden as cover, inching closer to the sleek silhouette of a black SUV. The gravel driveway posed a challenge, forcing the switch to my suppressed Glock for its stealthier approach. With muscle memory, I emerged from cover, my aim true as a single shot was fired, eliminating the lone guard with lethal efficiency.

Motioning for Kim to join me, I dragged the body of the fallen guard into the shadows, limiting any alarm being raised by his absence. With a nod of approval, she slipped into her SUV, the door closing with a faint but audible click.

I followed suit, sliding into the passenger seat as the engine roared to life, the thrum of the motor a relief as we made our escape into the night.

"How did they know we were there?" I asked Kim.

"How do people know where anyone is?"

"Do you have leaks?"

"If you are paid enough money, most people leak."

We continued our journey until Kim deemed it safe to pull over, making sure we remained at a safe distance from our intended target. Stepping out of the vehicle, we melded into the darkness, shadows becoming our allies as we advanced on the looming structure before us.

Pausing at a vantage point, Kim and I exchanged a silent glance, a wordless agreement to take in our surroundings before proceeding any further. With a sense of caution, we stopped, taking a moment to observe the building in its entirety, searching for potential threats or vulnerabilities.

"It looks quiet," I said.

We waited.

Nothing happened.

No guards, no movement, no anything.

"I'll go and have a look," I said to Kim. "If the proverbial hits the fan, you'd better come and get me."

"If it hits the fan, you'll probably die."

"Thanks for the vote of confidence."

Leaving Kim concealed in her cloak of shadows, I moved with silent determination toward the baleful edifice. A quick sweep of the perimeter revealed no visible sentries. Raising the hair on the back of my neck, exercising caution, I closed in on the rear of the structure.

At this point, I found myself contemplating the prospect

of a covert entry. With practiced subtlety, I checked the door, finding it unlocked.

Stepping over the threshold, I was immediately enveloped by an uncanny silence. The scent of a hastily abandoned meal lingered in the air, indicating the recent presence of inhabitants now conspicuously absent.

Navigating the dimly lit interior with cautious steps, I methodically cleared each room, my senses on high alert for any sign of life. Yet, to my annoyance, the space remained eerily deserted, proving how cunning Morozov, my quarry, really was.

Despite my best efforts, he had once again slipped through my fingers, leaving me with nothing but frustration and the daunting realization that our game of cat and mouse was far from over.

I made my way outside and found Kim where I had left her. "No one is there."

She nodded. "Then we move to the next part of our plan."

"Which is?" I asked.

"We go and see Min-Ho."

"Will he talk?"

"I can be very persuasive," Kim told me.

"Somehow, I think you'll need to be."

"I have a question," German said, interrupting. "Two, actually. Why didn't you go after the chips again, or just go to Cuba and continue the mission from there?"

"Because I thought it would be easier to intercept the chips in Seoul before getting to Cuba, where the country is being run by crooked politicians, a drug cartel, and Russian infiltrators," I pointed out. "I was determined to do all I could to stop them before they got there."

"Fine, please continue."

Min-Ho's establishment was no ordinary restaurant. It was a hidden gem nestled in the heart of the bustling city. Positioned strategically, it attracted a steady stream of foot traffic and curious tourists. The tantalizing aroma of authentic Korean cuisine wafted through the air, drawing hungry patrons like a magnet.

The restaurant buzzed with activity, its tables consistently filled each night. The ambiance was subdued and intimate, thanks to the soft glow of mood lighting that bathed the space. Along the walls, flickering candles cast dancing shadows, creating an enchanting atmosphere for diners to savor their meals. Min-Ho's culinary haven was more than just a place to eat. It was an experience, a taste of Korea wrapped in warmth and candlelight. It was a great front for the other things going on behind the scenes.

We were met by a maître d' at the front desk. Kim said, "Is Min-Ho in?"

"The boss is a busy man entertaining tonight," the man said.

"I won't keep him long," Kim said.

She stepped into the dimly lit dining room, deftly navigating her way through the tables toward the back of the restaurant. I trailed behind her, curiosity piqued about what she had planned. Our destination was within reach when a couple of unexpected obstacles materialized: two impeccably dressed men in suits, their stern expressions unwavering.

Kim's gaze darted past them. In the secluded corner, Min-Ho sat flanked by two men. But it was the trio of women who stole the scene. Elegantly attired, they exuded confidence and allure. Their purpose? To cater to the whims of the other men, to stroke their egos, perhaps, or to weave a web of influence.

"I'm here to see your boss," Kim said.

"Go away," one of the bodyguards said.

Kim pulled her weapon and drove the barrel deep into the man's stomach, doubling him over. His friend, panic etched across his face, fumbled for his own firearm.

But I was faster. My Glock materialized in my hand, its cold metal a reassuring weight. I leveled it at the second man, my finger steady on the trigger. His eyes widened, pupils dilating in fear.

With a smirk, I delivered my verdict. "Too slow, pal," I taunted, the words dripping with disdain. "You should practice more."

Min-Ho looked at Kim, a look of annoyance flashing across his face. He spoke to his men, and they hesitated. I guessed what he was saying, and I said to the man I was covering, "Fuck off."

I was aware of the eyes burning holes in my back, anxious to see if I would use the Glock or not. Min-Ho snapped out more words and the sea parted in front of us, permitting Kim and I to step forward.

The mobster gave Kim a cold smile. "My most favorite intelligence officer. I hear you had some words with your brother."

"It was a rather heated discussion," Kim allowed.

His gaze focused on me. "You'd be Mr. Kane. Yes?"

"I could be."

"It would seem we have a mutual friend."

"If you're talking about Gennady Morozov, then you'd be wrong."

Min-Ho nodded. "He suggested your friendship was rather hostile."

"You could say that."

Looking back at Kim, he asked, "So, what do I owe the pleasure?"

"You can tell us where Morozov is," Kim said.

"I don't know. He departed my hospitality shortly after word filtered through about what happened with your brother. You will have to kill him, you know?"

"You'd like that, wouldn't you?"

"Less competition."

"Where did Morozov go?" I asked him.

"I don't know."

I shook my head. "That's hard to believe. A man like you, with the connections that you have, would know a lot of things."

"Like who you once were? The people you worked with, that you have a sister. I know these things."

My anger surged. "Is that supposed to impress me?"

"I don't know, does it?"

"If it was a threat, you'd be making a mistake. If you know that much about me, then you also know the number of people like you that I have killed."

He stared at me, trying to figure out whether I'd just returned the veiled threat he'd leveled against me. In the end, he smiled wryly and said, "Be careful of your words, Mr. Kane. In my country, we pride ourselves on being polite."

"So, be polite. Where is Gennady Morozov?"

"I have told you, I do not know. I have not seen him."

Kim said, "Maybe you should think very hard, Min-Ho, just like me. I'm thinking of a certain warehouse with twenty million dollars of illegal imports in it. I'm also remembering another with one hundred million in cocaine. Plus, an additional shipment coming in tomorrow."

Suddenly, Min-Ho's face went pale, and he looked worried.

Kim smiled. "That got your attention."

The mobster swallowed hard. "Perhaps you are asking the wrong questions."

I nodded. "All right. Did he leave Seoul?"

"No. Come on, you can do better than that."

"Does he have the microchips yet?"

"No."

I was fast growing tired of the game of twenty questions. My Glock came up and pointed at his face. "Fuck it. I'll find him myself."

Min-Ho's hands came up. "All right, I'll tell you."

He glanced at his friends.

"I'm waiting," I said impatiently.

"Jae-sung is meeting him tomorrow at the old mill in the hills. The handover will take place there."

"What time?"

"In the afternoon."

"What about the scientist? Will he be there too?"

"No. He was sent on ahead to Cuba."

Accepting what he told us as true, I said, "Wasn't that easy?"

"Do not come back to Seoul, Mr. Kane. If you do, I will kill you."

"I'll remember that."

CHAPTER 4

AMID THE ROLLING HILLS OUTSIDE OF SEOUL, NESTLED WITHIN A secluded valley, stood the old mine mill. A relic in time, its worn wooden beams sagging under the weight of centuries. This was where the exchange would take place. The air hung heavy with moisture as a persistent drizzle covered the landscape in a soft gray mist.

I lay still, sensing the cool trickle of water coursing down the side of my face. Beside me, Kim remained motionless, both of us anticipating the arrival of the participants.

"I hate rain," Kim whispered.

"Yeah, me too. But we were taught to embrace it in the Recon Marines. It gave us an advantage, so they said. I just think we got wet."

The abandoned mill, once a bustling hub for grinding rocks into gravel, now stood forgotten. Overgrown and in disrepair, it cast a sad shadow on the landscape. The once-vast pit surrounding it had dwindled to a mere stain, a secluded spot where no one ventured. And so, it became the perfect location for their covert meeting.

The challenge lay in acquiring both the microchips and Morozov. Ideally, I wanted him alive, but the priority remained the microchips. In the distance, thunder rumbled, the leaden sky voicing its disapproval of our presence.

Glancing at my watch, I noted the advancing hour. Soon, twilight would wane, and darkness would envelop us.

The SR-16 lay beside me while the S&T Motiv K14 sniper rifle was also within reach. The next ten minutes saw the drizzle ease and the gray sky lighten a touch even though it was now late in the afternoon.

Then came the sound of the approaching vehicles. They appeared, bouncing through the slush and puddles of the muddy road. Three SUVs. They stopped and everyone remained within.

Kim said, "That is my brother."

"How can you tell?"

"I know."

Within minutes, two more vehicles arrived, their doors opening. The entire party alighted from the SUVs.

I picked up the sniper rifle. "Here we go."

Through the scope, I observed what was unfolding. It moved from Lee to Morozov. He'd brought seven men with him. Lee had ten.

Tucking the rifle hard into my shoulder, I targeted one of the men closest to Morozov. My finger took up the slack with the crosshairs on the Russian's head. Then, just as I fired, the air around us was filled with bullets.

The K14 slammed back into my shoulder and the round blew through the Russian's head. Meanwhile, we were taking heavy fire from our right flank. "Kim, lay some fire on that shooter."

Kim crawled around me, opening fire while I focused on another target below. This time, I turned my attention to the vehicles, rendering two of them inoperable.

Suddenly, one of Morozov's bodyguards lunged for the case containing the valuable chips. Lee swiftly pulled it back, but before I could react, Morozov drew his handgun and shot Lee in the head. The man crumpled, dropping the case to the muddy ground.

With precision, I adjusted the crosshairs of my sniper rifle, locking onto the bodyguard who had picked up the case. The trigger came back under my finger, and the .308 Winchester round hurtled toward him at nearly 3,000 feet per second. Impact. He collapsed, the case slipping from his grasp.

Morozov wasted no time, snatching up the case as I worked the bolt on my rifle, preparing for the next move. The chaos blurred in several moments of violence.

I wasn't quick enough and the Russian ducked behind the SUV. Searching for another target, I was about to fire when Kim said, "We can't stay here, John."

Bullets kicked up dirt around us and I knew she was right. I grabbed the SR-16 and said, "This way."

We ran through the rain, bullets chasing us. Kim and I found cover behind a clump of rocks and prepared for another onslaught of gunfire.

The shadows emerged from the trees further up a wooded slope. I aimed at the first one I saw and stroked the trigger. The would-be killer stumbled and fell, sliding forward on his face. A second killer fell foul to the accurate shooting of Kim, but almost immediately, they were replaced by another four killers.

That was when I noticed they were dressed differently to those who'd been below at the mill. These shooters were dressed in full combat kit. "It's Grigori Igoshin," I snapped, firing at another shooter. He ducked into cover, then opened fire.

"They're everywhere, John," Kim said, remaining calm.

She was right. We were taking fire from four different angles, and if we weren't careful, we'd get pinned down. "Move, I'll be right behind you."

Kim leaped to her feet and started running. I burned through most of the magazine in the assault rifle and then grabbed the sniper rifle before following her. Dropping into cover behind an old deadfall that Kim was sheltering behind, I reloaded the SR-16 and started firing once more.

"We have to get back to the SUV," Kim said.

"We have to get the chips," I replied.

"Forget them," she snapped. "We can try again later if we live. We have to get the fuck out of here to do that."

"All right, lead the way."

Once more, she was running, bullets nipping at her heels. I was close behind as we dodged and weaved through trees and brush. The SUV loomed up ahead, and then we were there, climbing into the vehicle, Kim starting the motor. She put it in gear, and we sped off, the rattle of bullets on its armored exterior the only sign they were still shooting at us.

I slammed my hand down on the dash. "Fuck!"

"We are not done yet," Kim said. "There is still a chance we can stop him from taking off in his plane."

"We have to find out from where."

The sudden appearance of two black Humvees behind us had Kim murmuring, "I think we have trouble."

Gunfire erupted from the pair of chase vehicles and peppered our armored SUV. Kim dodged and weaved the car, its rear end becoming loose on the slick, muddy road.

I wound down the window and leaned out, firing at the Humvees. Even though I hit them, the bullets failed to do any damage, ricocheting away harmlessly.

Kim took a sharp turn and the tires squealed on the street. Behind us, more gunfire erupted as the Humvees drew closer.

"Under the seat," Kim snarled wildly.

"What?"

"Under the seat."

I reached down and felt something solid. With a tug, it came free, and I was looking at a small case with combination locks and a handle. Kim said, "Six, three, six, eight."

"What?"

"The combination. Six, three, six, eight."

I punched in the numbers and the lock clicked open. Lifting the lid, I was staring at three fragmentation grenades.

"Never leave home without them."

"I know someone who would love you," I said, removing one from the molded base.

The pin slid out effortlessly, and I leaned precariously out of the window. With a calculated toss, I released it, hoping it would detonate beneath the front vehicle.

But it rolled forward after hitting the street, the impact making it detonate before the lead Humvee drove over it. Orange flames shot skyward, and the Humvee swerved wildly to avoid the explosion.

Muttering a curse, I tried the next grenade with better success. The explosion seemed to tear the front from the Humvee, and it stopped dead in a ball of flames. Behind it, the second Humvee took evasive action, swerving around the blazing vehicle, and started after us. I grabbed the last grenade and tried again. Not as successful as the previous one, the third grenade was sufficient to get the job done, blowing off the right front wheel so that the vehicle came to a grinding halt.

Our SUV sped on as we left the carnage behind us. I straightened in my seat and said, "We need to find where Morozov is leaving from. Now that he has the chips, he'll want to get airborne. They'll be headed to Cuba."

Kim spoke out loud and her cell connected a Bluetooth call. She spoke fast about something I couldn't understand. Both she and the woman on the other end went back and forth until the call ended.

"There is an airfield north of the city. A private jet just logged a flight plan to Cuba from there."

"That has to be it," I said as Kim sped up.

For the next twenty minutes, she negotiated traffic and Seoul's busy streets until we reached the perimeter of the airfield. Already waiting there for us was a contingent of ROK Special Forces commanded by Captain Park.

When we alighted from the SUV, he said, "We have snipers around the perimeter and eyes on the plane."

"What do they see?" Kim asked.

"The target is on the aircraft and the stairs are still down," he replied.

I frowned. "Guards?"

"Two."

"Something isn't right," I said. "We need to move in now."

I grabbed my assault rifle and started running. Behind me, Kim called out, "John, wait."

"We don't have time."

They all started following me, Park barking orders. Remaining in place, the snipers held their fire.

As I rounded the corner of a hangar, I brought my rifle up, pointing it in the direction of the nearest guard. "Put the weapon down!" I shouted in Russian. "Do it."

Both men looked in my direction, unmoved. "Drop them or I'll fire."

They looked past me and saw the rest of the assault force closing on our position. They placed their weapons on the ground and lay face down. Without missing a step, I started to board the plane.

At the rear of the plane, facing away from me, seated in luxury seats, was the man I wanted. "Gennady, stand up."

He never moved.

I lowered the assault rifle and brought the Glock up. I walked cautiously forward, the weapon aimed at the back of Morozov's head. "Gennady, stand up."

Again, he didn't move.

This time, I moved past him to stand in the aisle facing the man. His head was down, looking at the floor. Already, I could feel the weight of dread settle on my shoulders. Slowly, his head came up and the bitterness flooded through my veins. The man I was staring at was not Gennady Morozov. We'd been tricked.

The man smiled at me. "He said you would come. Hecate told him so."

"Fuck!" I stormed outside and down the steps onto the tarmac.

Kim saw the expression on my face and said, "The microchips?"

"Not here."

"Did you search the whole plane?"

"No, you don't get it. Morozov isn't here, neither are the chips. We've been tricked."

Morozov, along with the chips, was on his way to Cuba. Kim's intel people had him boarding another aircraft on the opposite side of the city. His ruse had worked, and we were once again behind the eight ball.

"What are you going to do now?" Kim asked.

"Follow him to Cuba," I replied. "I need to stop them from doing what they're planning."

"I wish you luck," Kim said to me.

"I have a feeling I'll need it," I replied.

Watching her walk away, I looked down as my cell buzzed. It was Holly. "I got your message, John."

"I'll leave for Cuba just as soon as I can. Can you reach out to the CIA and get me some help on the other end?"

She said, "I'll contact Ken Newman, the director. I'm sure they will help."

"Thanks. I'll talk to you later."

"Be careful, John. Cuba is a whole different world."

"Holly?"

"Yes, John?"

"Find out who the fuck Hecate is."

"So, it was you who initiated the contact with the CIA, Miss Smith," Holland said.

"Yes, it was. I knew Ken from Afghanistan. He was more than willing to help once he knew what was happening. In fact, he insisted on it being a joint operation. So much so that he shipped equipment into the region overnight. Then he organized for John to be inserted into the country to work with one of their officers on the ground."

"Yes, work, not murder him," Newman growled.

"Care to tell us what all that is about, Mr. Kane?" German asked.

I glanced at Christine Ryan. She nodded slightly. "Before you do, Mr. Kane, can you tell us who Hecate is or what it means?"

"I will get to that," I replied.

CHAPTER 5

I WAS CONVEYED TO CUBA VIA A SMALL AIRCRAFT FLYING BELOW the radar. Used previously by the CIA, the pilots flew missions to deliver deniable operators to the region. I didn't ask their names and they didn't ask mine. They'd done this before and knew exactly where they were going.

Below us was a lush green landscape of wondrous beauty. The type you saw in glossy brochures to make you want to travel there. But recently, the country had a dark underside. The new regime was a list of corruption, guided by the hand of Julio Garcia, the largest and only drug cartel leader in the country. He was like a god, and to succeed in my mission, I was likely going to come across him at some point. That brought us to the one and only condition of the CIA's assistance. If I did happen to encounter Garcia, they would take it as a great favor if I would—how did they say it —put him in the ground.

The plane dropped lower, hugging the earth as we approached the airstrip. Air turbulence made the aircraft bounce and I found myself thinking that if we hit a decent air pocket, we'd slam into the ground, and I'd be screwed.

"Five mikes," said the voice in my headset.

I looked out the window.

"Once we touch down, you need to help us unload so we can get out again."

"Copy that."

Off to my right, I saw a long scar in the green landscape. The single dirt runway was a leftover from the cartels of the '80s. Now the CIA used it for their operatives and running in supplies.

The pilot put the plane into a tight turn, making the machine stand on its wing as he lined the runway up. No sooner had he leveled it out when it touched down and bumped along the dirt strip.

The motor throttled down, and the plane turned on a dime. The copilot came back and opened the door. "All right, let's get this done."

The humidity was fierce as I stepped onto the runway, the gravel and dirt crunching under my boots. I had a Glock in a thigh holster and a Heckler and Koch 433 slung over my shoulder. Looking around, I saw there was no one there to meet me.

"Where's my contact?" I asked the copilot.

"Fucked if I know, pal. Our job was to get you and the supplies here. After that, it's all yours."

By the time the unloading was done, there was still no one there. I watched the plane take off, and minutes later, I was enveloped in the silence of the landscape.

After twenty minutes of waiting, the sound of several motors approaching could be heard. I grabbed up the 433 and jogged toward a line of thick undergrowth bordering the airstrip. Crouching down, I waited for the vehicles to arrive.

When they appeared, it was a truck and a Toyota van. They drove along the runway, kicking up a cloud of red dust before stopping next to the crates of supplies that had been on the plane.

Six people got out of the truck and started loading it. The van disgorged only two. The driver and a woman. Both were armed.

I studied them for a minute before showing myself.

"You looking for me?" I asked.

"You Kane?" the woman asked. She had dark hair and a slight Hispanic accent.

"Yeah."

"I'm Elana Sanchez, your contact on the ground. We should finish loading this up and get out of here."

I figured she was late twenties but not native to Cuba.

The truck was almost loaded when a radio transmission came through, and the news wasn't good.

"Elana, we have vehicles coming in."

"Who are they, Ramon?" she asked.

"Garcia's men. Three vehicles en route. Everyone is armed."

I worked the charging handle on the 433 and flicked the safety off. Elana called out to her men, and they grabbed their weapons, ready to meet the threat. Spreading out, they took cover.

"Are they reliable?" I asked Elana.

"They'll fight."

The incoming vehicles appeared, but no one opened fire. Elana brought up her AK-74 and waited. Once within the desired distance, everyone opened fire.

The cartel vehicles screeched to a stop, and shooters leaped out. Gunfire now erupted from them as well and bullets sliced through the air. I took up position behind the Toyota van and heard bullets punching into it.

An exposed cartel shooter fell to the ground as I fired the 433 at him before he crawled into cover. He may not have been dead, but he was certainly out of the fight.

Cartel shooters fell under the accurate shooting of Elana's men. We were gradually whittling them down, but it was taking a lot of ammunition, and before long, we had our first casualty. A shooter had exposed himself too much and took a round in his chest.

I saw him go down and left the cover of the van to check on him. His eyes were closed, and I checked for a pulse. Nothing to find. I glanced at Elana. "He's gone."

"Fuck."

Observing the position of my comrades, I recognized an opportunity to outmaneuver the cartel. Swiftly, I circled around, placing myself strategically. The moment was ripe, and I unleashed a torrent of fire upon our adversaries. They crumbled like a row of toppled bowling pins, and victory was ours.

As the dust settled, our forces surged forward, overwhelming the remaining cartel attackers. The battle had reached its conclusion, leaving no room for doubt. The echoes of gunfire faded, and the once chaotic scene now lay still.

Elana's men started to shoot the wounded. If permitted to live, they could pass on valuable intelligence.

I turned to her. "How did they know?"

"They would have heard the plane. Garcia has coca fields and a factory nearby. They would have come for a look. We need to get out of here now, before more come."

I climbed into the van and, pulling the door closed, we started off. She turned to me and asked, "Why are you here?"

"Didn't they tell you?"

"No."

"Not even the Brits?"

"No."

"The Russians," I said.

"What Russians?"

"Christ almighty. Do you people live under a rock down here?"

Elana turned and glared at me. "Our mission brief down here is the Garcia Cartel. That's it."

"All right. The Russians have R-12 ballistic missiles in Cuba. They are installing new engines in them. My mission here is to stop that from happening."

"I'll have to have a word with my station chief."

"Who is he?"

"Jack Carroll."

"Then let's do that."

"Not you. You will be staying elsewhere."

"Listen, I need to find five missiles. The quicker I do that, the quicker I can leave. In those supplies are the explosives that I need. There is, however, one other thing that your masters want me to accomplish."

"Which is?"

"Kill Garcia."

"You are fucking kidding?"

"No. I wish I was."

The conversation kind of dried up at that revelation, and the van continued driving along a gravel road. As we crested a hill, Elana got her driver to stop.

"Do you see that?"

I looked out the window. The undulating landscape stretched out before us. She continued. "They are Garcia's coca fields. And that is just a small sample. Last year, he shipped ten billion dollars in drugs to the US. This year, it is expected to double."

"So, what are you doing about it?"

"We are watching and passing on information while Garcia gets bigger and bolder."

"Hurry up and wait?"

She nodded. "Hurry up and wait."

Elana gave the order, and we started off once again until we reached a valley that was covered in tobacco crops, the edge of which had a high rocky ridge behind it, a plantation. We pulled up in front of the main house and climbed out. All around us were smaller buildings, dogs, and workers who went about their daily chores.

We were greeted by a middle-aged man and his wife, Alfredo and Maritza. They owned the plantation and were also CIA operatives. In fact, the plantation was a CIA cover.

"Mr. Kane, pleased to meet you," Alfredo said before introducing me to his wife.

"Pleased to meet you both," I replied.

The truck was unloaded, and everything hidden in a

basement beneath a large barn-type structure. Before Elana left, I said to her, "I need to find the missiles."

"I will pass it on to Jack. I will return after dark from Havana."

I nodded and then she left. I hated waiting.

———

While killing time, I shared a coffee with Alfredo. "How long have you been here, Alfredo?"

"It was my father's father who started the tobacco fields here," he said to me, gesturing with his hand. "I grew up in this very house."

"What about the CIA?"

"Ten years. They came to me when I needed money, and I could not refuse."

"Tell me about Garcia."

Alfredo shook his head. "He is a bad man. If anyone goes against him, he has them killed. And their families, to make an example."

I nodded. I had come across the type many times. "Why does he leave you alone?"

"We went to school together. At one time, you might even say we were friends."

"Does he have coca plantations in the area? Labs?"

Alfredo nodded. "Why?"

"Because I have been asked to eliminate him, if possible," I replied.

"I think they ask a lot of you, my friend."

I smiled. "You could be right. Now, have you heard anything about missiles in the area? Have your people seen anything?"

"No, but I can ask around. Someone will know something."

"Thank you."

———

When Elana arrived back, she was accompanied by a thickset man in his midforties. Jack Carroll had been in Cuba for five years and was staring down the barrel of another five.

We shook hands and he said, "Mr. Kane, Elana has informed me of your mission here. I'm sorry, but our resources are limited, so we will be restricted in any help we can provide."

"You do realize what is at stake here?" I asked him.

"Yes, I do."

"Have you ever heard of Stalin's Spear?"

"No."

"Let me give you the no-bullshit version," I growled.

Once I was done, he looked at me apologetically. "Like I said, we will give you what assistance we can, but don't expect too much."

"Then I'll do it myself. Starting with a little soiree tomorrow while I wait on intel."

"What do you mean?" Carroll asked.

"I have a lab to blow up."

"Wait a minute—"

"No, you wait a minute. I've got a job to do. Now, if you aren't going to help me, then stay the hell out of my way. I'll need Elana to help me with things. Are you up to it?" I looked at her askance.

"Sure."

"No," Carroll snapped.

"Then I'll make a call to Newman, and we'll see what he has to say."

The chief of station muttered something under his breath and said, "Fine, Elana can help you."

"I wasn't asking your permission." I looked at Elana. "Be ready to go in the morning."

"Typical Kane cowboy shit," Newman said to me.

"I was doing what you asked me to do," I snapped back at him. "It was Carroll who more or less refused to give me anything."

"He was told to help you, Kane."

"Well, he made it fucking difficult."

Early the following morning, I gathered the things I would need from the cache. I grabbed some C4 and a couple of detonators. I also took body armor and a couple of thermite grenades. I looked at Elana. "We need some accelerant."

"I can do that. I'll see Alfredo."

Elana was wearing jeans and a sleeveless T-shirt. I threw her some body armor and said, "Just in case."

Then I took a spare suppressed 433 and handed that to her too.

We loaded everything into the van and started off with one of Elana's men, Ramon, acting as a guide.

While we drove along the rugged track, I asked Elana, "What is Carroll's problem?"

"You mean apart from the fact that he's in charge of one of the most dangerous CIA stations in the world?"

"How long has he been here?"

"Five years."

"And he hasn't been replaced?"

"No."

"Someone must fucking hate him."

She chuckled.

"He doesn't seem very proactive. What does he do all day?"

"Checks reports. Studies surveillance photos, shit like that," Elana replied.

I grunted and looked out the window at the distant mountains. An hour later, Ramon pulled off the track into some trees far enough to be out of sight. He said, "We go the rest of the way on foot."

Scrambling out of the vehicle, we began trekking across the rugged terrain toward the lab. For thirty intense minutes, we pushed through thick foliage until the trees finally gave way, revealing a sprawling large coca field below. On the opposite side, nestled among the greenery, stood the laboratory.

I raised my binoculars and swept the area. There was no one in the field, but there were seven or eight workers around the open-air lab. Some were obviously armed. I guessed that the others were too.

"How do you want to do this?" Elana asked me.

"We'll use the coca plants for cover, and once we're close enough, we'll take them out and set the explosives." I looked at Ramon. "Once we secure the area, take that drum of fuel and spread it around. Before we leave, we'll set the field alight. Must be a few million here."

Ramon nodded. "I'll see to it."

Elana and I moved silently through the coca field, keeping as low as we could to avoid detection. Then, when we were within range, I called a halt. Elana stepped up beside me.

"Follow my lead. Leave no one alive."

"Okay."

I held up three fingers and then lowered them one at a time.

Three...

Two...

One...

Zero...

I stood tall, the 433 leveled and ready for action. My sights fell on the first target, and I fired three times. Single shots, close together. Red splotches appeared on his white T-shirt, and he fell to the ground. Another cartel soldier beside him acted surprised when he should have ducked. My next three shots killed him too.

Beside me, Elana opened fire with her own suppressed weapon. Her target fell and disappeared behind some crates.

I started walking forward through the coca field. A figure appeared with an AK. Two shots were enough to put him down but not enough to stop him from reflexively squeezing the trigger. The rattle of the AK rang out over the coca field like a warning to anyone within earshot.

Elana opened fire at another shooter and missed, her bullets shattering a plastic bucket on nearby crates. The man returned fire and bullets scythed through the air. I heard her growl, "Motherfucker."

She fired again, and the shooter fell backward out of sight.

I moved quickly and reached the lab. It was open air to allow fumes to escape. It had only a metal roof to keep the rain out. A cartel man emerged from a wooden privy and opened fire with a handgun. I felt the tug of a bullet on my clothing and knew I had come close to catastrophe. The 433 I had came to life and stitched a line of bullets across his chest, sending him to the afterlife.

There were two more shooters, but I had no idea where they were. I was sure I hadn't miscounted. Then I heard Elana call out. Emerging from the lab, I saw her pointing across the coca field at the two running men.

My weapon came up and I dispatched both before they could escape. "That should be all of them."

"There is a wounded man over there behind the crates," Elana said.

I glanced over to where she'd pointed. A cartel man was dragging himself away from the lab. Walking over behind him, I shot him in the back of the head.

"I'll get the charges set. Start Ramon burning what he can in the field."

For the next ten minutes, I set the charges and then met up with Elana and Ramon in the field. "Are we all good?"

"Yes," Elana replied. "But be aware, this is going to put the cat among the pigeons."

"Just what we want," I replied. "We want Garcia out in the open. Burn it."

Ramon took out a Zippo lighter and set the gasoline alight. Soon, flames were roaring through the field and a dark cloud of smoke was rising, a stark contrast against the cerulean sky.

Shortly after, I triggered the explosives, and the lab went sky-high.

————

"Well, you certainly kicked the fucking hornet's nest, didn't you?" Jack Carroll growled. "Garcia is going off his head. He's taking people off the street and killing them to find out what happened. Shit."

It wasn't what I wanted to happen, but doing this type of thing, you have to compartmentalize the good from the bad. "Put word out that there is a mercenary team living in the jungle that are working for a rival."

"I told you it was a bad idea."

"And I told you to stay the fuck out of my way if you weren't onboard."

"So many people are going to die because of this."

"Just do what I told you to."

It was then that Alfredo spoke up. "One of my men has located a launch site not far from here."

It was good news. "Show me on a map."

The plantation owner got his map and pointed out the location to me. The terrain looked rugged and secluded. "It looks like there is only one way in and out."

"Road, yes, but there is a path over the ridge behind it. It is steep, but it can be traversed. It won't be easy, but it is possible."

"Can one of your men guide me to the top of the ridge?" I asked him.

"Yes."

"I will go with you," Elana said to me.

I shook my head. "No, this one is something I must do alone. Go back to Havana and see if you can find out what is happening with the Russians."

"Okay," she agreed with a nod. I could sense a little relief in her tone.

I said, "I will go tonight."

Elana followed me outside onto the home's veranda. "You will be alright tonight?"

"Yeah. It's what I do. Plenty of miles on this weary frame," I told her.

"What are you going to do?"

"I'll take some explosives with me. Look around, see what I can find, and then blow the missile up."

"It will be dangerous."

"If what Alfredo says is true, they will be looking in the wrong direction."

———

I reached out to Holly. "We've got our first missile. I'm going in tonight to destroy it."

"Do you need a backup team, John?" she asked me.

"I should be right," I told her. "How are things on your end?"

"Let's say it's starting to get interesting."

"As in how?"

"The fifth general has appeared."

"Do you have a name for him?"

"Not yet. I've got Slick digging."

"And that other matter?"

"Working on it."

"What other matter are you talking about?" Holland asked.

"Nothing important just yet," I replied. "We'll get to it."

"How about we get back to the matter at hand," Newman said.

"I've no objection to that."

"I do," Christine Ryan said. "I need a bathroom break. Go and get some coffee. Be back here in twenty minutes. Does anyone object?"

"I don't think so," German said. "Let's take a break."

So, we took a break, headed for the canteen as usual, and had coffee. I stared across the table at Holly and asked in a low voice, "Any news from Hunt?"

She shook her head. "Nothing yet."

"Are you really going to pop him?" Knocker asked me.

"What do you think?"

He grinned. "What I think is that you're going to get what you need and dump him in the middle of Trafalgar Square."

I pointed at my friend. "You know, I hadn't thought of that, but you just might have something."

"Fuck, won't the Russians go off if he suddenly appears alive. Especially when they think he's dead."

Holly said, "For this to work, we need to produce him to the panel."

I nodded. "True."

"That way, we find out who Hecate is."

"We don't even know if it is one of them," Knocker said.

"That's why we need Lash to speak."

I looked at my watch. "Time to go back. Thanks for being here today."

"All good, Reaper. Let's do it."

We went back and took our places at the table. The others were already waiting for us. Christine Ryan said, "Welcome back. Now, tell us about that first strike and what happened next."

CHAPTER 6

THE MOONLIGHT BATHED THE LANDSCAPE, CASTING ELONGATED shadows across the rugged terrain. But it wasn't just the moon that held our attention. The incessant hum of bugs filled the air, their tiny wings beating against the silence of the night. Annoying, yes, but also a reminder that life persisted even in the darkest corners.

Our Land Rover sat abandoned at the base of the reverse slope, its engine ticking as it cooled while we embarked on our ascent. The ridge loomed ahead, its silhouette jagged against the night sky. The undergrowth clung to our boots, impeding our progress. The trail we followed was more of a suggestion than a well-defined path, disappearing into the foliage at times.

Even with night vision, I struggled with seeing the path, but Diego led the way. How he discerned the trail amid the chaos of leaves and branches was a mystery to me. Yet he moved with purpose, a steady rhythm to his steps as we climbed the steep incline. Each foothold was deliberate, each breath measured. The bugs buzzed around us, a persistent annoyance, but Diego remained unfazed.

Two-thirds of the way up, we halted our ascent. The wiry Cuban, seemingly impervious to exertion, showed no signs of tiring. As for me, my mountaineering skills were rusty, and my goat-like agility had waned. Each step felt heavier, my breaths labored. The summit loomed above, a challenge drawing us in. I glanced at the Cuban, his determination unwavering. Perhaps he was more goat than man, effortlessly scaling the rocky terrain. Meanwhile, I considered my own limitations, wondering if I could ever regain the grace of those nimble creatures.

"Are you okay, American?" he asked.

"Fine. Just not used to the climb."

"Going down will be easier for you," he replied.

"Let's keep moving."

Our ascent seemed never-ending, the summit never feeling any closer. Before midnight, we stood atop the rocky crown, our breaths mingling with the night air. The peak, adorned with jagged rocks and imposing boulders, seemed to defy gravity itself.

As we caught our breath, the thick underbrush parted, revealing a moonlit vista that held both promise and peril. I withdrew my binoculars, adjusting the focus until the missile site below came into sharp relief. Lights flickered, patrolling figures moved like shadows, their purpose inscrutable from this distance. I'd know more about what I was facing once I reached the valley below.

I turned to Diego. "This is as far as you go. Wait here until I return. If things go wrong and I'm not back by daylight, get out of here."

"I will be here when you return."

Diego's assertion proved accurate. The descent was markedly swifter than our arduous climb. I navigated the trail with care, my steps more assured than during the ascent. The moon, a fickle companion, played hide-and-seek with the drifting clouds. Its glow intermittently vanished, plunging me into shadow.

As I descended, the forest revealed itself, a combination of gnarled branches and rustling leaves. The night creatures stirred, their nocturnal sounds echoing eerily. A distant howl, a rustle in the underbrush.

When I reached the base of the ridge, I paused to revise my situation. The absence of a perimeter fence worked in my favor, providing an unguarded entry point. Yet, the ever-present Russian patrols—like elusive specters—loomed as a constant threat. Their movements were unpredictable and evading them required skill.

But then, there was a shift in the night's sounds. Spanish words, their cadence unfamiliar yet strangely comforting. For a fleeting moment, I entertained the thought that they might be Cuban military personnel.

Through the haze of white phosphorous night vision goggles, reality sharpened. The voices materialized, showing a motley crew of two emerging from the night. Not soldiers, but something more insidious. The cartel. Their presence sent shivers down my spine. I crouched low, senses alert, waiting for the next move in this dangerous game.

From the shadows, I swept the missile site and eventually found it hidden beneath camouflage netting. In my pack, I had three preprepared explosive charges. The first would be placed on the missile, the other two on targets of opportunity.

I slung the 433 and took out my suppressed Glock before breaching the invisible perimeter. Using whatever cover I could find, I paused frequently to maintain my security. Eventually, I reached the launcher.

Unshouldering the pack, I placed the charge right where it would work best. With that done, I was about to move when I heard a soft footfall close by. Turning slowly, I saw the shadow looming over me. Somehow, maybe by good fortune, he was facing the other way.

However, the risk of him seeing me was too great, so I placed the Glock on the ground and drew my knife. Moments later, my left hand was clamped over his mouth to keep his death silent, and my knife had already done its savage work. I lowered the guard to the ground and hid him under the launcher.

My next target was a military-type truck. I placed the

charge under it and moved along to the second truck. This one was a fuel tanker.

Common sense should have told me it was time to leave after that, but I paid no heed. Instead, in the search for more intelligence, I crept through the shadows toward a large canvas tent. Easing back the flap, I found it empty, although there was a lamp burning inside at a desk. Glancing around, I could make out no immediate threats and entered.

My main focus was the papers on the desk. I flicked through them and found nothing at first, but when I neared the bottom, I saw a map with positions marked. 8K63.

These were the other missile sites.

Taking out my cell, I took a couple of photos before putting it away. It was time to leave. I'd overstayed my welcome and that wasn't good. As I was about to find out.

There was movement behind me, and I turned swiftly to see a Russian soldier standing there. His jaw dropped in shock, contemplating the intruder in his midst. He drew in a deep breath to cry out a warning, and my muscle memory kicked into action. It was as though I was a gunslinger from an old cowboy movie and my Glock seemed to leap into my hand. It fired twice and the man dropped to the floor of the tent.

I muttered a curse. I'd solved one problem but created another. If he was found dead in the tent, they would know that someone had been in there, and maybe even seen the map, which might cause them to shift the missiles to new locations.

There was only one thing for it. The body had to be removed.

Bending down, I slung him over my shoulder. Luckily, he wasn't that heavy, and I carried him out of the tent and over to the launcher, managing to stay out of sight while I did it. I placed him beneath where I'd set the explosive charge, knowing it would mask the man's death.

I slipped out of the camp and started back up the ridge. About halfway up, I stopped and lifted my NVGs away from my eyes. Then I took out the detonator switch and pressed the button.

The small valley was shaken by the huge explosion, the orange fireballs lifting skyward, imitating the sun and casting light across the surrounding ridges. Eventually, the echoes of the explosions faded away.

One last look, and I continued climbing.

When I reached the top, Diego was waiting where we had parted company. "Your mission was successful, my friend."

"Just one of a few I'll have to complete before this is over, Diego," I replied.

He nodded. "We must go, I hear a helicopter coming."

I paused and listened. In the distance, I could hear the whop-whop sound of the incoming aircraft. "I hear it too."

We started down the reverse slope and, when we reached the bottom, climbed into the vehicle we'd arrived in. As we pulled onto the dirt road, I felt relief, but like I had told Diego, this was just the beginning, and things were only going to get worse.

―――――

Unknown to me at the time, the helicopter had a mercenary force on it. Grigori Igoshin was now in Cuba, and I was his number one target. Igoshin was ex-special forces and a cold-blooded killer. He'd served in different theaters across Africa and was wanted in The Hague for war crimes, having slaughtered a village on behalf of a Chinese mining magnate who wanted to get at the large deposits of diamonds beneath it.

After getting off the helicopter, he took one look at the devastation before him and said to one of his men, "Scouts out. I want to know what happened here."

He and six others were the advance force of what was already inbound: a further fifteen operators. Gennady

Morozov stepped up beside his hired man. "What do you think, Grigori?"

"It had to have been him," came the reply. "Once the rest of my people arrive, we will widen the search. Go back to Havana. We will handle this."

And that is what happened. Morozov returned to Havana while the mercenaries came searching for me.

But before they found where I was holed up, something else happened and drew me away from my current mission.

———

Upon our return, Alfredo's wife graciously prepared a delectable meal for me. The aroma of Cuban cuisine wafted through the air, enticing my senses. The dish was piping hot, and with each flavorful bite, I savored the blend of spices, tender meats, and fresh vegetables. It was a culinary delight that left me longing for more. The woman sure could cook.

"How did it go?" Alfredo asked as I took a bite.

"Fine. Mission accomplished."

"Diego?"

"He's a good man."

Alfredo nodded. "He is."

Once the meal was finished, I excused myself, headed for the shower, and went to bed. I slept deeply and my slumber was dreamless.

I was woken two hours later by Alfredo. He had a worried expression on his face. "John, wake up. There is a problem."

"What is it?"

"Come. Jack Carroll is here."

I rose from the cot and followed Alfredo to the living area of the plantation house. Carroll was pacing back and forth. He saw me coming and stabbed a finger at my chest. "You. This is your fault."

"What is my fault?"

"They have Elana. They picked her up an hour ago."

My blood ran cold. "Who?"

"If she hadn't been trying to impress you, they never would have found her."

"Who, Carroll?"

"Garcia."

"How?" I growled. "How did he know about her?"

Carroll shook his head. "I don't know."

"Where are they holding her?" I asked.

"An old police station in Havana," he replied. "Why?"

"I'm going there to get her out," I replied.

"It is suicide. Garcia's people roam the streets day and night. You would not last five minutes," Alfredo warned me.

"Then how does Carroll last?" I pointed out.

"That is different," Carroll said. "They are looking for you."

"If they look hard enough, they will find me," I said. "Have you ever heard the expression about catching a tiger by the tail?"

"I think so."

"If they're not careful, they might just catch one."

"I will send Diego with you."

"No." I looked at Carroll. "You can help me."

His eyes widened. "What? If I get seen, my cover is blown."

"Three words, Carroll. I don't care. Get ready to fucking leave."

———

Beneath the swaying palm trees and the vibrant façade of Havana's colonial architecture lies a covert underworld. The city buzzes with secrets, whispered in dimly lit bars where the scent of aged rum mingles with the acrid tang of cocaine. Julio Garcia relies on power. The power backed by the Colombian drug cartel. Their alliance is an unholy matrimony forged in violence.

Where most cartel leaders move through cities like

phantoms, Garcia was open and in your face. The crumbling streets of Old Havana bore witness to his empire. An opulent mansion, once owned by a sugar baron, now served as his home, while others served as drug dens. Once, the streets were covered with the slogans of revolution. Now faded indiscriminate graffiti marked the cartel's territory.

But he didn't have it all his own way. In the twisted alleys of Havana, where the humidity clings to your skin like a lover's touch, La Culebra weaved her web. Her real name was Dayani Mengana, simply known as The Snake. A smuggler and a survivor.

La Culebra's network stretched from the crumbling docks, where fishermen unload their catch, to the grand hotels where diplomats sipped mojitos. She slips vials of cocaine into cigar boxes, hides heroin in hollowed-out mangoes, and bribes customs officials with promises of forbidden pleasures. Her soldiers are exactly that. All former military. While Garcia and her had an uneasy truce, below the surface, there was a simmering hatred that one day would boil over.

It was this that I hoped to tap into and utilize. Besides, we were old friends, or should I say, enemies.

The ancient pickup slowed and then stopped outside an old colonial in a narrow alley. I turned to Carroll. "Wait here."

"This is a bad idea, Kane."

"I guess we'll find out."

The Glock was tucked into the back of my jeans as I climbed out and slammed the door. I walked up to the double gates and pressed the button.

"Who is it?" the voice asked from the speaker box.

"John Kane. I'm here to see Dayani."

"Who?" the voice asked.

"Tell her the Reaper is here to see her."

The reaction I'd been expecting wasn't the one I received. Six armed men with automatic weapons stormed the gate and stood there, guns pointed in my direction. With a nod, I said, "I see she remembers me."

Moments later, a slim woman appeared, her red dress hugging a lithe body, and her dark hair hung past her shoulders. In her left hand was a thin cheroot, and her right held a Beretta. Her coal-black eyes stared at me, her pretty face etched with displeasure.

"What do you want, John?" she asked in her husky voice.

"Still looking as good as ever, Dayani," I replied.

"I swore I would kill you when I saw you again."

"Well, here I am."

She spat a bit of cheroot onto the ground. "I can't believe I fucking slept with you."

"These things happen."

"Let him in," she growled. "The least I can do is give him a Cuba Libre before I kill him."

The gates opened, and I walked through. Two of her guards stepped forward. I said, "There is a Glock at my back."

They took the handgun, and I followed Dayani into her colonial home.

The sun, like a golden coin, filtered through the wrought-iron grilles of the tall windows, casting intricate lace-like patterns on the polished marble floors. The air hung heavily with the scent of aged wood and cigar smoke. It was a relic of a bygone era, a time when sugar barons and tobacco tycoons ruled the island.

As I stepped over the threshold, the grandeur of the place enveloped me. The ceiling soared impossibly high, adorned with ornate plasterwork that seemed to defy gravity. Chandeliers, their crystal prisms catching the light, dangled like frozen rainbows. The walls wore layers of faded wallpaper, peeling in places to reveal glimpses of the past—a floral motif here, a faded map there.

"You've done some work," I said, looking around.

"You noticed."

The central courtyard beckoned—a secret garden hidden

within the mansion's heart. A fountain, its stone cherubs forever frozen in playful splashes, stood at its center. Bougainvillea vines clung to the walls, their magenta blooms contrasting against the weathered ochre facade.

Rooms branched off from the central corridor like veins from an ancient tree. The library, with its mahogany bookshelves, held volumes of old leather-bound books.

In the dining room, a long table stood, its surface polished to a mirror-like sheen. Silver candelabras held wax-dripped candles. The chairs were upholstered in faded velvet, their once-vibrant colors now muted.

The bedrooms played home to four-poster beds with canopies draped in yellowed lace, while the ballroom was a cavernous space that had hosted dances and various gatherings long since forgotten.

As I stepped into the courtyard, Dayani ushered me to a chair around a small round table. "Sit."

I sat down, and no sooner than I had done so, a tall, thin man brought out two rum and Cokes. "Do you still drink it?" Dayani asked.

I nodded. "Yes."

"What about your friend? The English one, Raymond."

"He is working on something else," I replied.

"What about you, John? What are you doing here?"

"I need your help," I said truthfully.

"My help for what?"

Dayani's voice was even, calm. I'd expected her to throw my request back into my face, but I guess she wanted me to go through the motions before we got to that part. "Garcia has a friend of mine. I need to get her back."

"Her?"

"Yes."

"Are you fucking her?"

"What's that got to do with it?" I snapped.

"Are you?"

"No."

"Why are you in Cuba, John?" Dayani asked.

"I'm here about the Russians," I replied.

"The missiles?"

"Yes."

"I don't believe this," Holland growled. *"You divulged top secret intelligence to a known criminal."*

"I told her nothing she didn't already know. I needed her help."

"What else did you tell her?"

"Like I said, nothing she didn't already know."

"Why should I help you? After all, I did swear to kill you, John."

"Because it will benefit you in the long run, Dayani," I replied.

"How? How could anything you do benefit me?" There was more than a little sarcasm in her voice as she stubbed the cheroot out in the ashtray.

"Because before I leave Cuba, I will kill Julio Garcia."

"Ha, he will kill you and leave your head on a spike," Dayani almost exploded. "The man is untouchable."

"No one is untouchable, Dayani."

"And you want me?"

I shook my head. "No. Just some of your men. They are former soldiers."

"If you take my men, then you take me."

"I've already taken you," I replied. Suddenly, I felt like James Bond.

"Where is this woman?"

I told her. "She is there with Garcia's men."

"And you are sure you can kill Garcia?"

I nodded. "Eventually, yes. But if you do this, no one must be left alive. Nor can your people be identified."

"Fine. I will help you. Then you will help me."

"I'm already helping you, Dayani."

"Believe me, John, you will help me more."

CHAPTER 7

THE OLD POLICE STATION WAS ANOTHER OF THE ISLAND'S RELICS. Its walls, once imposing, now were dry and cracked by time and neglect. The iron bars in the windows were rusted, now a mottled orange, flaking away to reveal the weakened core beneath.

Inside, the air was thick with the mustiness of decay. The narrow corridors echoed with cries of Elana's pain. Cells were lined up on either side of a long hallway. Small beams of moonlight filtered through the cracks in the ceiling, casting eerie shadows that danced across the floor.

Outside in the darkness, a block away from the jail itself, we prepared for the assault. I would lead, while Dayani and her handful of former soldiers would be close behind. There were three guards patrolling the exterior of the old police station. How many were inside, I had no idea. We'd do a sweep and secure it. Carroll had left me with the cartel woman and gone back to his safe house to wait for news.

"Are your people ready?" I asked Dayani.

"Yes."

I pulled the lower half of my mask up and nodded. "Let's go."

We were strung out in a line. As I said before, I led the assault, my suppressed 433 up and ready. I hugged the wall where the moonlight couldn't reach, stopping at the intersection where the derelict building sat opposite. Two of the guards were near the front door. The other must have been patrolling around the rear.

Stepping out of the shadows, I pressed forward. My finger stroked the trigger and the first cartel soldier fell. My aim changed and the second man died as well.

Using hand signals, I indicated for two of Dayani's men to head around back. They would take care of the third guard.

I stepped aside and the next man up hit the door. It flew back and we entered. Almost instantly, a cartel shooter appeared. He died where he stood, bullets tearing into flesh and bone.

We pushed through what used to be the front reception area and stopped at a closed door. One of Dayani's men hit it and went through, followed by two others. Gunfire rattled from within, loud in the enclosed spaces.

By the time I entered the old cell block, it was over. Every member of the enemy had either been taken down or taken prisoner. Elana had also been located, tied to a long table where she had endured all manner of torture.

Her body was a pitiful sight. She'd been beaten, sustained cigar burns on her exposed skin. Three fingers on her left hand had been removed, and she had been electrocuted numerous times. Turning to Dayani, I said, "Get her out of here."

As the cartel boss hovered over her, she looked up at me. "John."

"What?"

"She's dead."

"Horseshit, I heard her scream before we came in."

"I'm sorry, John."

Three men were on their knees near the wall. I stalked over to them, my fury and frustration at having arrived too late simmering just below the surface. "Who did this?"

They shuffled on their knees but kept their gaze fixed on the floor.

"Who told you to do this?"

No one answered.

Unwilling to play their game, I pulled my Glock, shooting the first one in the head. As his body toppled, I changed aim and sent the second one to hell, just to prove to the third that I wasn't bluffing.

"Stand him up."

Two of Dayani's men dragged the remaining cartel soldier to his feet. I pressed the Glock under his chin and said, "Who ordered it?"

"It was Julio. It was him."

"Why?"

"Because he wanted to know who blew up the lab."

"What did she say?" I asked.

He shook his head. "Nothing."

"How did Garcia know about her?"

"H-he knows everything," the man stammered.

"Fuck off. How?"

"The American. He tell Julio that she was working with the CIA."

"What American?" I snarled.

"The one with the woman's name."

Carroll!

"Lies!" Newman exclaimed. "You're lying to cover your own fucking ass. You got my niece killed, you cowboy son of a bitch, and you know it."

"I never got her killed, Newman. It was Carroll. When we dug into him, we found a separate bank account with ten million dollars in it. Garcia had been paying him off for a while. Yes, everything was fine until I arrived, but that was only because he was station chief, and he could control the situation. You asked me to do a job. I was doing that job when Elana was betrayed and tortured to death."

"She was helping you."

"She knew the risks. And so did you when you posted her

there. She was a strong woman. Her not speaking under duress proved that. I was sorry about what happened to her, but it wasn't my fault."

"What John says is true," Holly said. "We looked into Carroll and found the money. We also found out that the money started being deposited around the time he asked to be transferred out of Cuba, but the request was denied."

"Are you saying it was the CIA's fault?"

"Not at all. Just circumstance."

"Are you sure it was the American?" I asked the cartel man.

"Yes."

"Fine," I said with a nod, pulling the trigger.

———

We took Elana's body with us back to Dayani's. When we arrived, she said, "My people will take care of her properly."

They buried her in a cemetery in a more upmarket part of Havana.

Dayani presented me with a glass of rum, served neat. I downed it in one swift motion before signaling for a second. As the liquid fire warmed my insides, the dawn began to break outside, its gentle light dousing the stars' dominion, bringing an end to the night's embrace.

I sat in a leather chair, my boots up on what was possibly an expensive coffee table. My host, who had been in the shower, now emerged wearing very little. Lacy black bra and panties to match. She walked over, took the empty glass from my hand, and then straddled my lap, making herself comfortable.

I felt the pressure as she forced herself against me. Dayani leaned in and kissed my lips. "Now I know why I slept with you."

"Why's that?" I asked.

"Because watching the way you conduct yourself in battle turns me on." She slapped me across the face.

"What was that for?"

She tried to do it again, but I blocked the blow and returned the favor. She grinned at me. It was almost maniacal. Then I came to my feet, taking her with me, carrying her to the big four-poster bed that was calling out to us.

"What about the shower?" she asked.

"Fuck it."

It was Dayani's people who brought Carroll to me. He was babbling about what was happening and demanding to know what was going on. They forced him onto a chair in the courtyard. My stare was hard, cold.

Dayani stood off to one side, keeping her distance. Carroll looked at me and said, "What the fuck is going on, Kane? Did you get Elana?"

"Elana is dead, Jack."

"I knew you would get her killed," he snarled.

"No, Jack, you got her killed. I know all about you and Garcia."

"What the hell are you talking about?"

"You know, Jack. One of Garcia's men talked. Now the question is, what are we going to do with you?"

"You're a fool if you believe anything the man said."

"Maybe," I said and shot him.

Dayani said to me, "What will you do now, John?"

"Go back to my search for the missiles," I said to her.

"What about Garcia?"

"I'll deal with him when the time comes," I replied.

She nodded. "I will take you."

I gave her a suspicious look.

"Your secret will be safe with me. Whoever is helping you, I will swear upon my mother's grave that they will be safe from my people."

Her promise may have been sincere, but my friends were far from safe. The pall of dark smoke staining the blue sky attested to that. As we entered the valley, the reason for it became clear. Alfredo's plantation had been destroyed, attacked with such violence that it was almost leveled.

Dayani eased her vehicle to a stop atop the gentle rise, and we disembarked to a vantage point overlooking the smoking ruins. I raised the binoculars to my eyes, scanning the desolate tableau that lay before us. The remnants of fires flickered amid the fallen, painting a grim picture of the aftermath. My gaze then settled on Alfredo, suspended from an improvised gallows, his form bearing the harrowing signs of torment.

I grabbed my HK433 and started forward.

"What are you doing?" Dayani asked me.

"I need my things."

"They could be down there waiting."

"I hope they are."

The scene was one of horror, strewn with lifeless bodies and the telltale remnants of Russian-made ammunition casings. As I cautiously navigated through the wreckage, each step heavy with dread, my senses were assaulted by the acrid scent of blood and smoke.

My progress halted abruptly as my gaze fell upon a fresh, muddy bootprint etched into the earth. Kneeling beside it, I felt a chill crawl down my spine as I recognized the distinct pattern. These were the imprints of Russian-made boots.

However, the presence of such boots in Cuba spoke of a clandestine operation—Russian soldiers would not be so overt in their maneuvers. No, these were the footprints of mercenaries, agents of chaos unleashed by the elusive Grigory Igoshin.

The name sent a surge of anger through me, for it carried the weight of countless atrocities. Grigory Igoshin, the merciless murderer, had once again spread his reign of terror upon the innocent.

This time, however, there stood someone ready to defy

the darkness, someone willing to stand up against the tyranny and fight back for the souls unjustly claimed by Igoshin's brutality.

I turned and faced the movement behind me. Dayani asked, "Was it Julio?"

Shaking my head, I said, "No. Russian mercenaries. Grigori Igoshin."

"I do not think I have heard of him."

"You don't want to."

Gently, I lowered Alfredo's lifeless body beside his wife, their hands almost touching in a final, silent farewell. The grim scene spoke of a fierce struggle, with remnants of Alfredo's followers fallen in futile surrender, their lives brutally claimed.

With a heavy heart, I turned my attention to what remained of the barn, its once sturdy frame now reduced to smoldering wreckage. Digging through the debris, I uncovered the entrance to the basement, remarkably intact amid the chaos, a testament to its stout construction and fireproof design. I retrieved what I needed with a sense of urgency, leaving the rest untouched.

A flash from a distant ridge caught my attention. "We're being watched."

Dayani nodded. "I thought I saw a flash earlier."

"Do you still want to help me?"

"Are you going to kill Julio?"

"More so now than ever."

"Then I will help you."

"Right, let's go," I said.

After we climbed back into Dayani's vehicle, she drove off, heading up the road. But once we'd gone a short distance and crested the hill and moved out of sight, I said, "Pull over."

"What?"

"Just pull over."

With a frustrated huff, she did, and I climbed out. I took my weapon and said, "Go down there and wait."

"John—"

"I'll be fine."

Dayani kept going, and I walked into the undergrowth and waited.

Not that I had to wait very long. The sound of an approaching vehicle reached my ears as I prepared.

Moments later, it crested the rise, and I stepped out onto the gravel road and unloaded a full magazine through the front windscreen. The white pickup truck swerved off the road and into a tree. I dropped out the empty magazine and reloaded, while walking toward the truck.

The two men in the vehicle were slumped forward, dead. My accurate fire had done what it was supposed to do. I checked to make sure they were dead, then went through their pockets looking for ID. I didn't find any, but their tattoos told me what I needed to know. They were Russians. Grigori's people.

Finding an encrypted cell, I threw it into the undergrowth and then walked away from the truck.

"Who were they?" Dayani asked me when I climbed into her vehicle.

"Someone you don't need to worry about."

———

Hours later, back at Dayani's old colonial home, I said to her, "I need to find the other missiles."

"My people can help you."

I took out my phone and showed her the map I'd photographed. "I just need to get to these."

Dayani studied them and said, "Start with that one."

"Great. There is another thing. I need to find this man." I showed her a photo of Morozov. "If he's here, I need to know where. There is a scientist with him who needs to be eliminated as well."

"What is all this about, John?"

"An operation started long ago called Stalin's Spear."

She frowned. "What is Stalin's Spear?"

"Back in the time of the Missile Crisis, it was the name the Russians gave to the plan where they had the missiles in Cuba. They were meant to have been taken away. Some were. The rest were hidden. Now they are refurbishing the engines so they will fly again."

"But why?"

"We think it has something to do with making the old Soviet Union whole again. We figure that with missiles in America's backyard, the Russians are hoping they will stay out of anything in Europe."

"Do you think they will?" Dayani asked.

"I doubt it. The scary thing is that Lash is just crazy enough to push the world over the edge."

"And that is why you're here. To stop it?"

"Yes. If I can."

"Then I will help you to stop them, John. For I, too, believe that this is foolish. It will only lead to Cuba being destroyed and many deaths."

"More deaths than you are involved in?" I asked her pointedly.

"That is business. That—"

WHAP-WHAP-WHAP!

Dayani died as three bullets smashed into her back. She grunted with each blow and slumped to the floor. I dived for cover behind the sofa as more rounds were incoming. I dragged the Glock from my jeans and opened fire at a figure standing in the doorway to the hall. The first missed, punching through the wall near the doorjamb. The next two found their target: the first hitting his chest plate and the second tearing through his throat.

The deafening crash of shattered glass broke the eerie silence, jolting me into action as another shadowy figure leaped through the window, landing perilously close. Reacting swiftly, I rolled to evade the incoming threat and unleashed a barrage of gunfire, the sharp crack of my weapon echoing through the room as my bullets found their mark. The assailant faltered, dropping his weapon with a clatter as he staggered backward.

With steely resolve, I steadied my aim, homing in on his form. As he struggled to regain his composure, I adjusted my sights, the weight of my courage heavy in the air as I delivered the final, fatal blow, a single shot piercing the chaos and finding its mark squarely on his face.

The room erupted into a cacophony of muffled gunfire, the staccato rhythm of suppressed weapons filling the air as the confrontation intensified. Amid the chaos, I took the opportunity to pick up the fallen assailant's weapon, my large fingers engulfing the cool metal of the AK-12 as I prepared to face whatever dangers lay ahead.

I came up and fired at another figure standing in the doorway which led through to the dining room instead of the hall. The rounds from the AK-12 hammered into the shooter and he disappeared.

My predicament seemed impossible, the relentless onslaught of enemy fire closing in. With dawning realization, I glanced over my shoulder at the shattered remnants of the window behind me, cursing under my breath at the circumstances.

"Son of a bitch."

Summoning every ounce of determination, I dropped the AK-12 and sprang into action, hurling myself through the opening with reckless abandon. The impact with the unforgiving ground on the other side was brutal, sending shockwaves of pain coursing through my body as I tumbled and rolled to absorb the force.

Gasping for breath, the world spinning around me, I fought to regain my bearings, gritting my teeth against the searing pain radiating from every bruised inch of my body. With a guttural groan, I forced myself upright, a wave of dizziness threatening to overwhelm me as I stumbled forward, desperate to put distance between myself and the lethal threat lurking within the confines of the building.

The ongoing staccato of gunfire drove me onward as I

sprinted desperately across the garden, my heart pounding in time with the destructive rhythm. The imposing stone wall loomed ahead like a fortress of fleeting safety, its jagged surface designed to prevent intruders.

With a surge of adrenaline-fueled determination, I hurled myself toward the barrier, the rough texture of the gravel biting into my palms as I scrambled for purchase, hoisting myself over the edge, the sharp edges cutting into my flesh as I tumbled to the other side.

Hunched over in a crouch, I heard the bullets hammering into the wall behind me, the whizzing of projectiles over-head a deadly reminder of my narrow escape. Taking a moment to catch my breath, I remained low to the ground, instinctively seeking out the cover of shadows that promised concealment.

With a silent prayer for stealth and luck, I darted to the left, my movements fluid and purposeful as I sought out any refuge amid the web of danger that surrounded me.

"Motherfucker," I growled stupidly as a figure appeared to block my path. He was armed and the weapon was sweeping around to fire.

Closing the gap as swiftly as I could, I blocked the sweep and thrust my Glock forward. I squeezed the trigger multiple times before the mercenary fell away to the ground.

Then I ran. Not knowing what else to do. My equipment was lost and so was the remaining hope of help to get my mission accomplished. I would have to regroup and come up with something else.

———

"I have a problem," I told Holly over the phone.

"You and me both," she replied dryly. "Tell me yours."

"I've lost all of my equipment, I've lost all of my contacts, the only other person who was going to help me is dead, and I've still got missiles to destroy."

"Fuck, John, does trouble just love you?"

"I just need a place to start," I replied.

"Okay, wait for my call. Are you safe?"

"For the moment."

"Fine, sit tight."

Seeking refuge beneath the sheltering expanse of a bridge, the musty scent of damp concrete and stale air enveloped me, a spectral whiff of the countless others who had sought solace in its shadows before me. As I huddled in the darkness, my senses alert to the faintest stirrings of movement, I spared a moment to consult the map displayed on my dwindling cell phone screen, the battery indicator flashing a warning of its impending demise. I put it to sleep to conserve power.

Next, I pieced together a plan. A vehicle would be essential, a means to navigate the rough terrain and evade pursuit. With determination, I knew I had to acquire one by any means necessary.

Weapons were next on my mental checklist. Though armed with a handgun, I recognized its limitations when facing the imminent threat. I needed to lay my hands on additional armaments.

Yet, it was the pressing need for explosives that played heavily on my thoughts, an essential component required to complete my mission.

My cell rang.

"Yeah?"

"I'm going to send you an address. Go there and wait. If nothing happens within the next twenty-four hours, you're on your own."

Then the call disconnected. My cell buzzed, and an address appeared. My next challenge was getting there.

CHAPTER 8

THE STREETS WERE BUSY, AND IT TOOK ME A WHILE TO REACH MY destination. It was another old colonial that MI6 used out of Havana. It had been unoccupied for the past month, but it was tidy. I'd been there ten minutes when I heard a knock on the door.

My hand dropped to the Glock as I approached the wooden barrier. I paused, stepping to one side. "Who is there?"

"Maria. Let me in."

I frowned, unlocking the door to a thin-faced woman wearing a floral dress. Carrying a bag of groceries, she stepped past me and entered the house as though she lived there.

"Who are you?"

"Close the door and I will answer your questions."

I looked outside the house, shut and locked the door, then followed her to the kitchen. She placed the groceries on the counter and turned to face me. She was young, probably in her early twenties. "Okay. This is the only time you will see me. I told you my name is Maria, that is the name I use. You will not see me again."

"What do you do?" I asked.

"I bring your food."

"Thank you," I replied with a nod.

"I am to tell you to expect visitors in the morning. Until then, you are to sit tight and wait."

"Who are the visitors?"

"I do not know."

"You don't have a phone charger in that bag of goodies, do you?"

Astonishingly, Maria reached inside and took one out. "It should be universal. I think of everything."

"C4?"

She reached into the bag again, then stopped, grinning.

I nodded. "You had me there."

"Now I will go. The longer I am here, the more chance there is of being discovered."

"Thank you, Maria."

"You are welcome. Good luck."

She took her leave, and once more, I was alone.

————

My new friends were British. SAS flown in from the US, where they were on exercises with the SEALs. Cramer, Hooky, Ted, and Shorty. They were the names provided and I asked no more. "The name is Kane," I told them.

Although Cramer was their commander, each man was treated equally. Cramer said, "Mind telling us what we're doing in Cuba?"

"What were you told?" I asked him.

"Head shed told us fuck all. Put us on a plane with some equipment, and here we are. All I can tell you is we're to blow shit up. Judging by the C4 we were given."

I nodded. "Yes, but there is a little more to it than that. The mission involves blowing up some R-12 missiles, assassinating a Russian general, and then doing the same to the local cartel boss."

Cramer nodded slowly. "I think they sent too many blokes."

We went over the map that I had a picture of. Cramer looked at Hooky and said, "You're our specialist on Cuba. You know this area?"

"Yeah. I can get us there."

"All right, we'll leave after dark tonight. You good with that, Kane?"

"I'm good."

Cramer looked at me thoughtfully. "Hey, aren't you that guy that Ray Jensen always talks about?"

"You know Knocker?"

He nodded. "Sure, I do. Mad bastard is always singing your praises. Good mate to have in a jam."

"Wish I had him now, actually," I replied. "No offense intended."

Cramer nodded. "Don't worry. We're just as fucking mad."

"You'll need to be."

———

Just before it got dark, we geared up and headed out. Each of us was armed with 433s, except for Shorty. He was our resident sniper and was using an M110A1 sniper outfit. We all packed C4, just in case. Hooky drove, getting us out of Havana without any problems. The plan was to not return, to live out in the wild until the mission was complete.

The SAS boys brought with them a sat phone. And it was about now that we had an incoming call. Cramer answered and passed it to me. "It's for you."

"Kane."

"What the fuck did you do?"

It was Newman.

I told him about Carroll and what had happened to Elana. At the time, I didn't know he was her uncle. However, I could tell that he was holding something back.

"Did you not think to tell Mr. Kane about that fact?" Christine Ryan asked.

"I didn't think he needed to know."

"But you blamed him for her death."

"And the murder of Agent Carroll."

"Yet you still helped him."

"Because he had other ideas in mind," I explained. "He still needed me, but he also wanted me on the hook."

Newman looked at his hands on the table. "That's correct."

"What do you mean?" German asked.

"I wanted him dead."

"And you tried, too," I said.

He looked up at me. The anger that he'd held over the past few days was gone. "Just as hard as I could."

"Continue, Mr. Kane," German said.

Arriving at our disembarkation point, we quickly concealed the SUV amid the rugged terrain, making sure our approach remained undetectable. With the vehicle safely stowed, we continued our journey on foot, the weight of our mission heavy upon our shoulders.

We ascended a steep ridge, each step was labored. When we crested it, we were met with an expanse of brush-covered landscape below.

Yet, as our gaze swept over it, a sense of dread gripped us. There, nestled beneath the concealing veil of a huge camouflage net, lay the silhouette of the R-12 ballistic missile, its presence a stark reminder of the danger it presented.

I passed the night vision capable binoculars to Cramer. "I can see ten guards. They look like Russian regulars."

He swept the area, looking for himself. "But how many can't we see?"

———

We paired up and left Shorty on overwatch. I took Ted with me while Cramer had Hooky. Ted and I would take the missile. Through a quick discussion between Cramer and myself, we decided to send a message to Morozov and his people.

In the distance, jagged bolts of lightning illuminated the sky, a prelude to the impending storm brewing on the horizon. With each flash, the darkened clouds churned ominously, the wind sweeping the front in from the coast.

As we huddled in anticipation, the air thick with humidity, we felt the first tentative raindrops begin to descend, the gentle patter against the earth a precursor of the deluge to come.

Timed to the rhythmic cadence of the rain, we embarked on our mission, navigating through the darkness provided by the veiling curtains of water. Each movement was purposeful and deliberate in the face of nature's fury.

Guided by the flickering illumination of the distant lightning, we pressed onward, our concentration unwavering despite the relentless wind and rain.

I dropped to a knee at the edge of the perimeter, trying to find that first guard I knew was there.

The rain came down in earnest, hitting the earth and pooling into ever-increasing puddles. The air crackled with electricity as bolts of lightning pierced the blackened sky, momentarily casting an ethereal glow upon the expanse of the missile site and the dense foliage of the surrounding jungle.

In the stark brilliance of a lightning flash, my gaze caught a glimpse of movement amid the shadows—a lone guard, cloaked in the obscurity of the night, standing vigilant against intruders. With a surge of adrenaline coursing through me, I instinctively raised my assault rifle, finger poised upon the trigger, as I braced myself for the coming confrontation.

Lightning flashed, and with it, every nerve seemed to be on edge. I steadied my aim.

I fired.

The target jerked and fell to the ground with a muddy

splash. Ted touched my shoulder, and I moved forward, breaching the invisible perimeter.

Out of the watery gloom, another soldier appeared. Once again, I fired, and the target fell. Behind me, meanwhile, Ted kept vigilant, sweeping left to right in an arc of 180 degrees.

Another shadowy figure appeared, but this time, it was the sniper setup of Shorty that spoke. Over the comms, I heard his low voice say, "You can thank me later."

The torrential downpour gradually eased to a mere drizzle, offering a momentary reprieve from the deluge. Through the haze of rain, the silhouette of the missile materialized before us, resembling a sleek cigar resting on its platform. With a subtle gesture, I signaled to Ted, beckoning him forward to initiate the placement of the C4 explosive. Meanwhile, I positioned myself strategically, ready to provide cover and support, ensuring our mission proceeded seamlessly amid the lingering threat of rain and danger.

It took the SAS man a few minutes, but the C4 was soon in position, and he joined me where I was crouched.

"All good, Kane."

I nodded. "Bulldog One to Bulldog Three, copy?"

"Copy, One."

"We're set over here."

"Right, get out. RV at the jump-off point."

"Roger."

We pulled back, using the rain for cover. Once in position, I hit the bang button.

———

As the next day dawned in our camp, dew dripped steadily from the verdant canopy above, mimicking the patter of raindrops. Nestled beneath the protective cover of foliage, we found respite from the previous night's deluge, grateful for the sanctuary that kept us dry.

Hooky came to Cramer and me with a screen he'd been

using to keep up with what was happening in the outside world. "We have a problem."

We looked at what he was watching. It looked like Garcia's men were taking people off the street, or executing them in public.

"They seem to be led by that guy there," I said, pausing the feed. The man I was referring to had on a white T-shirt and striped pants and was covered in tattoos. His hair was shaven, and he was escorted by two bodyguards. "Find out who he is."

"Roger that."

Cramer looked at me. "What are you thinking?"

"That we take him off the board. Let Garcia know that he or his people aren't untouchable."

"It could escalate things."

"I guess we'll find out. In the meantime, we need to locate the next missile."

An hour later, Hooky came back to us. "I have him."

CHAPTER 9

"His name is Andy Delgado. Former Cuban Army. Sadistic prick who enjoys his own special kind of torture," Hooky explained. "The type of asshole that would look better with a bullet hole in his forehead."

I nodded. "Good work. All we have to do is find him."

"He has a place in Havana. Lives there with his family."

"What family?"

"Wife and kid. From the intel I've gathered, she was the daughter of a tobacco farmer. Just took her for himself."

"Fine. Let's free her from her shackles. You got an address, Hooky?"

"Yeah. Let's get this prick. Have a look at this."

He showed me pictures of some of the damages the killer was responsible for. The man was an animal and didn't deserve to walk the earth with decent people.

We prepared for a night infiltration. However, before leaving camp, Hooky came to me with another problem.

"Kane, I managed to get a satellite retasked to check out all of these missile locations. The problem is, they're not there."

"What?" I couldn't hold back my surprise.

"They've been moved."

"Fuck it."

"Look, I'll see if I can come up with something, but we're going to need another source just in case."

"Like who?" I asked rhetorically. "Everyone to do with this thing is a fucking ghost virtually."

"Not everyone," Hooky said. "Not this guy, anyway."

He showed me another picture. It was a Russian general in full uniform. "Who is he?"

"General Maksim Kokorin. Special adviser to President Sergey Lash. If anyone knows where the missiles are, it will be him."

"If we take him, we need to be prepared to have the whole island searching for us," I pointed out.

"Cramer has a box of tricks that might come in handy."

I called Cramer over and discussed our predicament, telling him what Hooky had said. The SAS commander nodded and asked, "What were you thinking, Hooky?"

"Have another look at this photo. The general is in it with a younger woman. Not his wife, it would seem, so I think we can safely assume that he likes the ladies. If we could pay a prostitute to act as a honey trap, we might be able to pump some of your juice into him and get what we need."

"You mean drug him?" I asked.

"That's it," Hooky replied. "That shit that Cramer has wipes the memory as well. Just like having a heavy night on the piss."

"And he won't know?"

"Not fucking likely," Cramer replied with a wry grin.

"All we have to do is put the plan into action."

"You leave that to me and Hooky," Cramer said. "You think you can do Delgado with Ted and Shorty?"

"Should be able to," I replied.

"Then let's do it."

————

Under the cover of darkness, we slipped into Havana, looking for the address of Garcia's gunman. The streets were far from quiet, but our luck held for the most part. That was until we were stopped by a pair of cartel soldiers who were manning a checkpoint within two klicks of our target.

They stepped out in front of our van, and I grabbed my suppressed Glock. Ted did the same. They approached the van from either side. I said in a low voice, "Take it easy, gents. Let's see what happens."

The windows came down and the cartel guy on the driver's side asked Ted, "What are you doing?"

Ted held up his fake press badge. "We're BBC press."

"What are you doing here?"

"We are doing a story, mate."

"On what?"

"Tobacco."

The man stared at us, his eyes flicking back and forth suspiciously. Then he said, "Show me."

"Show you what?"

"Show me film stuff or I kill you."

"Come on, mate, I showed you my ID."

"Get out of the van." His demeanor had changed markedly. "Get out now."

Bringing his weapon up, he pointed it directly at Ted. On my side, his companion did the same. "Ted," I said. "Show him your new hand-operated camera."

"Yes, Boss."

The moon hung low in the sky, casting elongated shadows across the deserted street. Our breaths were shallow. The mission had escalated quickly, and now we found ourselves backed into a corner.

Our weapons, sleek and deadly, rose silently, barrels aimed through the opening. The shots popped through the night and both men fell backward, their bodies crumpling onto the street.

We hurriedly alighted from the van, boots crunching on street grit. The air smelled of the ocean, but death hung heavy on the breeze as well. One of the fallen men groaned, his eyes wide with shock. We leaned in, methodical and efficient. One shot each—center mass. No second chances.

As their lives slipped away, their breaths gave a final rattle. Dragging their bodies into the shadows, we were certain they would remain undetected, at least until morning. The street remained deserted, the world blissfully ignorant of the violence that had unfolded here.

Back in the van, the engine purred to life. Ted once more took the wheel, and I settled into the passenger seat. Our mission wasn't over yet, though. Delgado awaited. As we drove away, the moon watched, its pale face indifferent to our deeds.

"That could have gone better," Ted said.

"Could have gone worse too," I replied.

Ten minutes later, we pulled up into the shadows along the street from the target house and waited. "What do you think, boss?" Shorty asked me.

"You and me will go in while Ted keeps overwatch from here." I passed him an earwig and put another in my ear. "How's that?"

"Sounds good."

We grabbed our suppressed 433s and hurried toward the house. It was cloaked in darkness, and I guessed that Delgado thought he was safe enough. There was no evidence of any guards. Maybe no one was stupid enough to go after one of Garcia's main men. But that was before MI6 and the SAS came knocking.

Scaling the low fence, we paused for a moment, looking around for any sign of danger. Moving quickly to the back of the house so we could access the rear door without being observed from the street, we had failed to factor in the possibility of our target owning a dog.

Luckily not a big dog, but a little barking annoyance that was persistent and would wake everyone up.

"Shoot the fucking thing," Shorty hissed in a harsh whisper. "It'll wake every bastard up."

I didn't want to shoot it, but we needed the little mongrel to stop. My 433 came up, and a sixth sense must have warned it something was about to befall it because it turned and ran, disappearing into the dark yard.

But the damage was done. A light came on, and through a window, I saw a shadow moving about. Shorty and I crouched low and waited to see what would happen. I heard a voice around the back. A man yelling in Spanish.

Using hand signals, I directed Shorty to follow me. We moved fluidly to the corner of the house, and I peered around. Standing on the back steps was a shirtless man covered in tattoos and holding a large handgun.

Delgado was summoning the dog to come to him, but there was no sign of it. He was facing away from us, so I knew I had to act fast. Outside was better than inside. The 433 in my hands came up and I hurried forward, my footfalls muffled on the grass.

The suppressor touched the back of his head and I said, "Drop the gun, motherfucker, or I'll paint the yard with your fucking brains."

"Do you know what you are doing, American?" he asked confidently.

"I have a good idea. Now drop the gun."

But the killer had stuff between his ears that was the opposite of brains. So, instead of dropping the gun, he tried to fight his way out of it. My 433 fired three times and Delgado died at his back door.

"Time to go," I said to Shorty.

Retreating along the route we'd entered by, we left the killer where he'd fallen. Once in the van, Ted said, "All good, boss?"

"Yes, let's get out of here."

———

Our small group reconvened at the safehouse where I'd first encountered Maria. Cramer told me that everything was in order for the following night, and all we had to do was wait for the signal. I looked at him curiously. "You managed everything?"

Cramer nodded. "Right down to the lady we're going to use to get our man."

"Who?"

"Maria."

"No." She was young, and I preferred not to put her in that position. Especially for the fact that once we were gone, she was on her own. "Find someone else."

"Listen, I know you have reservations, but we don't have any time for Plan B. It's her or we do it another way."

I didn't like it, but he was right. "Okay, we use her, but I want to talk to her first."

"Don't you trust me, Kane?" Cramer asked, a hint of indignation in his voice.

"I do, but it doesn't change my mind."

"All right. I'll arrange it."

True to his word, he had Maria come in. I studied her for a moment before I spoke. "So much for not seeing you again."

"Things change," she replied nonchalantly.

"My friend tells me you are going to help us."

Maria nodded. "Yes."

"Have you thought it through?" I asked her. "If you do this, it could make you and your family a target for the cartel or the Russians."

"I have no family."

That gave me an idea of how to secure her future. "If you do this, you must leave Cuba."

"And go where?" she demanded as though I was exiling her from her home.

"To England."

"Whoa, Kane, we don't have the authority to do that," Cramer rightfully reminded me.

"I'll get authority," I assured him. "Either she leaves, or we don't use her."

The SAS man saw the compromise and agreed. "All right, we'll do it your way."

My gaze settled on Maria once more. "Well?"

"You can do that?"

"I can do that. You'll have a place to live and a job."

"Then, yes, I agree."

"Give me a moment." I took out my cell and made a call. "Hello?"

The voice on the other end was a woman. "It's me."

"John?"

"Yeah."

"It's been a minute."

"I need a favor," I said.

"Of course you do."

"I have a young lady who is about to help us with something dangerous. I need a way out of Cuba for her, along with all the trimmings. Job, place to live, and money."

"How much money, John?"

I looked at her. "A couple of hundred thousand."

"Christ, John, you're asking a lot."

"She's risking a lot. Once this is done, she needs a new life."

There was a sigh followed by, "All right, leave it with me."

"Thanks, I'll buy you dinner the next time I'm in London."

"You'll be doing a lot more than that, I can assure you."

The call disconnected, and I saw the astonished expression on Maria's face. "You just did that?"

"Yes."

"I don't know what to say."

"Just get out of this alive. That's all I ask."

———

The plan was essentially straightforward—though with a hint of complexity. The Cuban government had organized a function for that night, to be attended by influential figures from across the country. Among the guests was Julio Garcia. However, there was about to be a wrench thrown into the mix, but I'll get to that soon.

Cramer, along with his associate, arranged for Maria to attend the soiree. We discreetly provided her with an earwig device, allowing us to stay in contact and monitor the situation. Positioned nearby in our van, fully equipped, we were ready to act should the need arise. Additionally, we had a helicopter on standby in case of an emergency evacuation.

Through the earwig, we could hear every detail. Maria also carried an inconspicuous camera, virtually undetectable.

She stepped into the opulent mansion, her emerald-green dress a striking contrast against the polished marble floors. The neckline plunged daringly, revealing just enough skin to captivate without crossing into immodesty. The fabric clung to her curves, accentuating her silhouette, while the hem gracefully brushed the floor. As she glided through the grand reception area, chandeliers casting a warm glow, her presence commanded attention. Guests turned to watch, their murmurs hushed in awe. Beyond the reception, she entered a cavernous ballroom, its high ceilings adorned with intricate frescoes.

"I'm in," she whispered, her voice soft, almost childlike.

"Just relax," I said to her. "We're here for you."

"Easier said than done."

The ballroom glittered with crystal chandeliers, the air thick with cigar smoke. High-ranking diplomats, politicians, and businessmen swirled in a waltz of power. Among them, General Maksim Kokorin stood—an imposing figure in his pressed uniform, his eyes like shards of ice.

Maria moved across the room with grace, her dress moving like an external skin. She had closed half the distance when Julio Garcia appeared in front of her, taking Maria completely by surprise.

"What a lovely flower you are, my dear, like the brightest hibiscus among these thorny roses."

Maria swallowed hard. In my mind, as I listened, I urged her to focus. She went to speak but her throat had constricted. "I—"

"Are you all right, my dear?"

"Y-yes, you just took me by surprise," she managed to get out.

"I am sorry. But I am wondering if such a beautiful woman like yourself would dance with a lowly peasant like me."

Maria grinned at Garcia. "I would hardly consider you a lowly peasant."

"Ah, so you know who I am," Garcia said.

"I would have to be dead not to. Julio Garcia, the great entrepreneur and supporter of the people."

He smiled back at Maria. "I see you are a master at stroking a man's ego. Is that all you can stroke?"

"I'm sorry, senor, but I guess you will never find out," she replied as she stepped around him and kept walking toward Kokorin.

"Well done, Lass," I heard Cramer say. "You handled that well."

Maria had studied Maksim's file—the man who brokered treaties with foreign nations, laundered money, and left a trail of bodies in his wake.

As the orchestra played a haunting melody, Maria approached Kokorin. Her smile was practiced, her eyes betraying nothing.

"Mr. Kokorin," she said, her voice a velvet whisper. "May I have this dance?"

His gaze swept over her, assessing. "You're not like the others," he replied. "What game are you playing, my dear?"

"No game," Maria said, her fingers brushing against his. "Just a desire for something…more."

He hesitated, then led her onto the dance floor. Their steps were measured, their bodies close. Maria's pulse quickened—she was inches away from her target and things were moving fast.

Beside me, Cramer said, "That's one way of doing it."

"The lure was too much for him," I replied.

"Tell me," Kokorin said, his breath warm against her ear, "what do you desire?"

"Escape," Maria whispered. "Away from this opulence, this suffocating world. A place where one can be oneself."

His eyes narrowed. "And just who are you, Miss—"

"I am called Maria," she whispered seductively.

"I must say, your offer is very appetizing," Kokorin said. "If indeed it was an offer?"

"You would be amazed at what I can offer."

His grip on her waist tightened. "What do you propose?"

"A midnight rendezvous," Maria said. "Away from prying eyes. Trust me, it will be worth it."

He studied her, suspicion warring with curiosity. "And if I refuse?"

"Then you shall go back to your hotel room and be alone and be awake all night wondering about what could have been," Maria murmured.

"What if you were to come with me?" he asked, his brown eyes glittering with lust.

"I'm sure that could happen."

As the waltz ended, Maksim nodded. "Lead the way, my dear."

Maria guided him through to the garden, beams of moonlight dappling the path. She knew we waited in the shadows, ready to extract her if things got out of hand. But Kokorin was no fool.

"Why?" he asked, stopping abruptly. "Why me?"

"Because I like to live…dangerously." A finger trailed down his cheek. "Don't you?"

Maria traced his leg up to his crotch and squeezed gently. She felt the general harden and said, "Look for me at midnight."

Kokorin hesitated, then leaned down and kissed her. It was a desperate, dangerous kiss. "Until then, Maria."

As he disappeared inside, Maria watched him go. The first part of the plan was done. Now it was up to fate to determine the outcome.

And as everyone knows, fate can sometimes be a fickle bitch.

CHAPTER 10

"DID ANYONE ACTUALLY APPROVE THE OPERATION YOU WERE conducting?" German asked me.

"I did," I replied.

"What about your handler?"

"My handler was thousands of miles away and I had neither the time nor the inclination to bother her."

"But that wasn't your choice to make, Mr. Kane," Holland pointed out. "There is a chain of command for a reason."

I looked at Christine Ryan.

She cleared her throat and said, "We encourage our agents in the field to make decisions when timing is crucial."

"What about offering the girl what he did?"

"That never came through me."

"Then who?"

"Anesha Perera," I supplied.

"The minister?"

"That's right."

Anesha was one of the youngest MPs in the British government at thirty-one. I had come across her for the first time in Myanmar. I was there on an operation when some internal strife kicked off. I managed to get her out of the country after she was kidnapped by extremists. Our relationship flourished from there.

Holland sighed, "So, once again, we have a rogue operative

conducting an operation in which the SAS are involved, and they're planning to kidnap a high-ranking Russian official."

"It was better than the alternative," I replied.

He frowned. "What alternative?"

"If things had been different, I would have killed him."

That was the moment that everything changed. Maria had returned to the soiree, and through her camera, I caught a glimpse of a familiar face across the room, a glass in his hand.

"Maria, turn back the other way," I said to her, wanting to make sure.

She did as I asked.

"Stop there."

"What is it?" she whispered.

"The man across the room from you. Have you ever seen him before?"

"No, should I have?"

"Possibly not."

"Who is he?" she asked.

"Gennady Morozov."

"What do you want me to do?" Maria asked.

"Wait one."

Cramer said, "You can't do it, Kane. We need to stick with the plan."

"We can get him," I said to Cramer. "He's literally right there."

"And if it goes wrong, we lose them both," he said, being the voice of reason.

I knew that he was right, but the urge to get him now was almost overpowering. I wanted him brought in, dead, hung up by his balls, it didn't matter. I wanted my pound of flesh.

"Kane," the SAS team commander said again.

I nodded. "It's okay, Maria, continue your mission."

"Copy."

I turned to Ted. "Give me an earwig."

"Oh, Christ," Cramer groaned.

I removed my combat kit and grabbed a jacket from my gear. Slipping into it, I tucked the Glock inside my pants. Ted handed me an earwig and I placed it into my ear. "This is a fucking bad idea, boss."

"It probably is, but I have to do something."

"You're going to fuck it all up," Cramer reminded me.

"I'll do my best not to." I did not look back at them, so I missed the dismissive eye-rolls of each member of the team.

Climbing from the vehicle, I closed the door quietly. Keeping out of sight, I ran through the shadows. Behind the building, I found the rear entry. There was a guard stationed at the door who appeared to be Russian. I watched him for a moment and reassessed it. I needed to get inside, and to do that, I would have to deal with the guard.

If I killed him, the alarm would possibly be raised by someone who missed him, completely blowing the mission. So, I came up with a plan. Walking up to the door, I said to the guard, "Tell Morozov I want to see him."

In my ear, I heard Cramer say, "Oh shit."

The guard looked at me strangely before turning and disappearing inside.

I said, "Cramer, make sure Maria is okay. And be sure to get her to England."

"You sound like you aren't coming back, Kane."

"Just in case."

A few moments later, after placing the earwig into my pocket, Morozov appeared, his bodyguard and Garcia in tow. He stared at me and then looked around. One of his bodyguards handed my Glock to him.

Then Morozov said, "I know you are up to something, Mr. Kane, but what is it?"

"I thought I'd say hello, Gennady. It's been a while."

"Not long enough. Was it you who destroyed the missiles?"

I smiled. "I've been busy."

Garcia stepped forward and slapped me across the face. I

tasted blood inside my mouth as a sharp tooth-edge cut flesh. "Was it you who killed Delgado, American scum?"

I mumbled something, and Garcia moved closer. Too close if you were him. My fist didn't travel far, but the cartel boss felt it. As he staggered backward. One of his men moved to intercede, drawing his weapon.

My bunched fist hit him in the throat, crushing his larynx. He went down too, falling to the ground, gasping for breath. The color of his face changing from red to purple. I said, "If you want him to live, I wouldn't waste any time in getting him to a hospital."

The remaining Garcia bodyguard dragged his friend away for medical attention. Morozov stared at me. "What is your purpose, Mr. Kane?"

"I'm here to kill you, Gennady. And to stop Mikhail."

"Not if I kill you first."

"Do you mind if we talk somewhere, just me and you?" I asked.

"No," Garcia snarled. "I am going to kill him."

"After," Morozov said, waving a dismissive hand at the cartel boss. "All right, Mr. Kane, follow me."

———

He led me into a room with overstuffed chairs and intricate tapestries. We sat down while the others remained outside. Morozov nodded and said, "Well, what are you going to waste my time with?"

In the transition, I had replaced the earwig, which meant I was now in contact with Cramer and his team again. "I'm here to tell you to give up on this idea you have. The missiles won't work."

"If you say so."

"We already destroyed those on Wrangel. We know about Hecate. We—"

"Stop," German said. "You haven't said anything about Hecate. You said you would get to it…them…whatever they are."

"Hecate was another deep cover operative we had to deal with," I said.

"Had to?"

"Yes. We believe the person that is now locked away is that person."

"Okay, continue."

"We know about Hecate and Dolos. We are slowly dismantling everything Shatov has implemented. Lash is trying to put the old USSR back together, but the world has moved on from all that. We also know Lash is trying to honor the memory of his grandfather, who was one of the original founders of your organization."

Morozov slow-clapped me, and I suddenly wished I had my Glock so I could shoot him in the face. "Bravo, Mr. Kane. Please continue."

"We figure that you are trying to use the missiles in Cuba to shackle the US from becoming involved when you roll across the frontier. Except it won't. But Lash knows that and will use it to widen the war. That leaves the UK. You need them to stay out of it to try and isolate the European countries. We're still working on that."

The grin on Morozov's face remained. "I can see why Mikhail is so fascinated with you and your friend. I think he wishes that you were working for us. I guess we're past bringing you over to our side."

With a shrug, I said, "Even if I agreed, you wouldn't believe me."

It was then I saw something in his eyes. It looked like uncertainty. Then he surprised me by saying, "What would it take?"

"What?"

"What would it take for you to abandon your foolish ideals and come to work for our great organization?"

"Like I said, you wouldn't believe me."

"There would be a period of adjustment. And we would want something upfront to prove your loyalty. So, what?"

"Fifty million."

"Kane, what the fuck are you doing?" Cramer asked, finally speaking over our comms.

I ignored him and stared at Morozov.

The Russian said, "Oh, come now, Mr. Kane, I thought a man such as yourself would ask a lot more than that."

"Fine, seventy-five."

"That is better. Now, what about your offer to us?"

Cramer said, "Kane, talk to me. What are you thinking?"

I said, "Out in the ballroom, there is a woman called Maria. She is wearing a green dress—"

"Fuck you," Cramer said.

"She is here targeting Kokorin."

A fleeting look of alarm crossed Morozov's face before he regained his composure. Standing up, he adjusted his jacket nonchalantly, then strode purposefully toward the door and disappeared.

"Cramer, you there?"

"What the fuck—"

"I don't have time. You'll just have to trust me. Don't do anything. Just let it play out until I tell you otherwise."

"I hope you know what the fuck you're doing."

When Morozov reappeared, he looked troubled. "We shall soon find out if you are as good as your word."

"My word is good. I can't be certain about yours."

He shrugged. "I wanted to kill you, but Mikhail may have been right to put his admiration in you. Either way, I win."

"Garcia might have something to say about that," I pointed out.

Morozov nodded. "Unfortunately, he is a necessary evil for the time being. I do not agree with the things that he does, but he has certain qualities. Eventually, we will have to kill him, but not just yet."

"Clean up after yourselves, yes?"

"Something like that."

A few minutes later, four people appeared. Two were Russian, one was Garcia, and the last was Maria. With a frightened look on her face, she stared at me. "John, what is happening?"

I walked over to her, took out her earwig, dropped it to the floor, and crushed it. She was shocked. "John, no!"

I hit her. Open handed but solid enough to make it convincing. Maria dropped to her knees. I turned to Morozov. "Is that enough?"

The Russian shook his head. "No."

One of his men stepped forward and took out his weapon. He handed it to me. I looked at Morozov. "What's this for?"

"You cannot trust him," one of the new Russians said.

"Quiet, Grigori," Morozov snapped. He looked at me. "You will now shoot her."

Maria's eyes widened. In my ear, I could hear Cramer speaking, but I was trying to block it out as I thought. "Why?"

"I think you know why, Mr. Kane. And if you try anything, my men will kill you."

I looked around. The man who'd handed me the gun was holding another. His companion also held one. It was one of those moments where everything was on the line. I was looking for a way to infiltrate the organization, which would get me the answers we desperately needed. On the other hand, I was about to kill an innocent person. A person who had placed her trust in me, trust that I had promised to keep her safe. Now I had to decide whether to shoot her or not.

So I did the only thing I could. With Cramer shouting at me in my ear, I shot her.

There was no crash from the handgun. No violent buck in my hand. There was nothing at all. I looked at Morozov. "Do you think that I would give you a loaded weapon? Not even with one bullet."

Just as I predicted it would be, it had been a test. I had gauged the weight of the weapon. A trained operator can tell the difference between an empty and loaded one. The bodyguard reached out and retrieved the weapon from me. Morozov said, "Take her away."

"My men will take care of her," Garcia said.

The Russian waved him away. "Fine, fine."

"Where are you going to take her?" I asked Garcia.

"We have a place where we deal with special cases."

"The old school?"

He smiled. "You have heard of it?"

"Yes." And now Cramer and his men had as well.

"We'll take care of it, Kane," I heard Cramer say.

Garcia said, "Soon, you will join her, American."

"No, he will work for us."

"That is a mistake," Igoshin snapped.

"I agree." Had the cartel boss been eating, I'm sure he would have choked.

"I have a task that needs completion, and I believe he is capable of accomplishing it."

"What might that be?" I asked.

"Well, since you are responsible for everything that has happened, it seems only fair that you should be the one to correct it. You will go to America and bring us something back."

"What?"

"The head of the director of the CIA."

"You're serious?"

Morozov sighed. "What is the best way to confuse your enemy, Mr. Kane?"

"Scramble his intelligence."

"That's right. The best way to do that is to cut the head off the snake, as you Americans like to put it. That is what we shall do."

"You want me to go to Langley and assassinate the director of the CIA, cut off his head, and bring it back here?"

"No."

"What do you mean, no?"

"Newman will be in Arizona. A small town on the border where there have been some major drug smuggling issues.

However, a leak was orchestrated regarding the possibility of a high-value package entering the country in that area. The CIA director and a small team are currently en route to Retribution Arizona."

"Fuck me."

Morozov frowned. "Is there a problem?"

I shook my head. "No, not at all. How am I getting in?"

"Julio's people will get you in. They will hand you over to one of the Mexican cartels and they will get you and the team under the border."

"What team?"

"Julio will supply a team to go with you to make sure that you accomplish what you need to."

I glanced at Garcia, and it was evident that if he had his way, I wouldn't be returning. With a deliberate nod, I acknowledged the unspoken tension in the room, knowing my next move would be crucial. "Okay."

"Until it's time to leave, you shall remain here. Do you have any further questions, Mr. Kane?"

"What about weapons?"

"They will be supplied to you once you leave."

With that, the small group filed from the room, leaving me to contemplate the position I'd put myself in and to come up with a plan.

"Things just took a huge turn, Kane," Cramer said in my ear.

"Yes. Just make sure you save Maria and get her out of the country. You know what to do."

"What are you going to do?"

"Follow through, come back, and get the rest of those missiles from the inside."

"Don't you have another way?"

"No. This way, we get the missiles and I get Morozov and Garcia. Good luck, I'll reach out when I return."

"It won't be me who needs luck," he muttered.

"What was the significance of the town in Arizona?" German asked.

"That's where it all started," I said.

"What?"

"Team Reaper. It was there that I ran across Juan Montoya."

"Never heard of him."

"I'll tell you sometime."

German looked at Newman. *"Mr. Newman, would you tell us about this operation?"*

"We obtained intelligence that a Saudi national, whom we'd been surveilling for some time, was about to cross the border to assume leadership of two terror cells. Our decision was to apprehend him before he could carry out his plans. As Kane so aptly put it, this operation was a deliberate trap to ensnare me. Our small but efficient team proved to be sufficient for the task."

"When did you realize that something was wrong?" Christine Ryan asked.

"When I saw Kane in Retribution with the cartel men."

"What were your first thoughts?"

"That I was going to kill the traitor no matter what."

German nodded. *"All right, let's continue."*

CHAPTER 11

UNDER THE CLOAK OF DARKNESS, I WAS TRANSPORTED AWAY from the humid embrace of Cuba aboard a military aircraft. My company included a dozen members of the Cuban cartel. Each one was a walking arsenal, a former soldier turned mercenary, with monikers that could have been torn straight from the pages of a gritty crime novel—El Carnicero, La Rata —The Butcher, The Rat. It was almost comical, their choice of dramatic aliases, as if they'd watched one too many American crime dramas during their downtime. Yet, the humor of the situation was lost on me, for beneath those nicknames lay cold, calculated killers, men who had danced with death so often it had become their leading partner.

Our journey took us to the heart of Mexico, where we were herded like contraband into the back of a nondescript truck bound for the border's dusty embrace. The Mexican cartel's foot soldiers eyed me with a mix of curiosity and contempt—a hulking American anomaly in their midst. The Cubans, too, regarded me with a wary gaze, their hands never straying far from their weapons. I could sense their trigger fingers itching, each man seemingly eager to add another notch to their tally.

In this game of spies and shadows, trust was a luxury none of us could afford, and I knew that my life hung by a thread, one that any of these men would sever without a second thought.

The Russians had supplied me with an AK-12, body armor, and ammunition. Attached to the weapon was a laser sight, and we also carried night vision capability.

Coming to a stop at a deep, dry wash, we climbed out of the truck and fell into two ragged lines. We were then escorted down into the gully and over to a tunnel, the mouth of which could be seen in the dry bank.

"What's this?" I asked.

"It will take you to the other side of the border," one of the Mexicans said.

"What's on the other end?"

"Another man with a truck. He will take you to Retribution."

"Are the CIA people there?"

The Mexican nodded. "They arrived just before dark."

"What if they try to radio or call for help once we engage?" I asked.

"You have got until three to get to the town. At that hour, all communication will be cut until noon, or until your return."

"What do you mean by all communication?"

"There will be no communication at all."

"What about us?"

"None."

End of conversation.

Walking into the mouth of the tunnel, I ducked my head to avoid hitting the string of lights that illuminated the long, straight passageway. Apart from the Mexican cartel guide ahead of me, I was leading the group through. As we walked, I found myself wondering how many people had walked the sandy ground beneath my boots.

When we emerged on US soil, we were greeted brusquely by an American with a flatbed truck covered by a tarp. He was a big guy, even in the dark, and I found out his name was Larry.

"Are you Kane?"

"Yeah."

"Get everyone on the truck and I'll take you to Retribution."

"Do you know what's happening there?"

"The CIA spooks warned everyone to stay inside for the night."

"Everyone?" I asked.

"Everyone that's left," he said. "There's say fifteen, twenty regulars plus our crew."

"What do you mean, our crew?"

"We run the distribution from there," Larry said.

"Who is we?" I asked him.

"You're asking a lot of questions." He turned to face me, hands on hips.

"It helps to keep me alive," I replied. "Not knowing can get you fucking killed."

"So can asking questions," he growled.

He walked off and it wasn't until he walked through the headlights that I glimpsed the patch on the back of his leather jacket. The guy was a biker.

It made sense. Bikers had far-reaching tentacles, which enabled a greater distribution network. It was common across the globe. What concerned me most was what the patch represented. I shook my head. "Just fuck."

He was part of The Reapers. They were an Arizona club based in Phoenix. In my time with Global, we'd come across them. Their president had been a vicious prick who was eventually convicted of torture, murder, trafficking of drugs and people, and numerous other offenses. His successor had immediately reached out to the cartels and implemented a new pipeline. And what better place than Retribution after Team Reaper had shut it down the first time?

Knocker hadn't been with us back then. In the beginning, the team consisted of Cara and myself. It was Luis Ferrero who put the rest together. Since the team's inception, there had been comings and goings, the latter mostly not by choice. We lost some good people.

Now I had bikers as well as the Cuban team to deal with. It was becoming more tenuous by the minute.

Once we were loaded onto the back of the truck, we started our jarring journey to Retribution.

———

It was two o'clock by the time we arrived. The moon was full, and the surrounding desert was bathed in a silvery sheen. Had the situation been different, I might have enjoyed the ethereal landscape. But Larry flipped back the tarp and growled, "This is it. You walk the rest of the way from here."

Climbing down, I turned and noticed the lights in the distance. We were maybe two miles from the town. Standing, I stared at the lights. "Something wrong?" Larry asked.

"Once we start, there might be a problem with your friends."

"We already thought about that," the biker said to me. "Which is why we're going to help you."

"What?"

He nodded over my shoulder. I turned, and not sure how I'd missed them in the moonlight, I noticed ten figures standing off to the side.

Yes, growing worse by the minute.

"You got a problem with that?" Larry challenged me.

My mind worked quickly as I analyzed the situation. With a shake of my head, I said, "No, just as long as you understand that I'm in command."

"Sure."

"We'll split them up. One of your guys with one of mine. Probably safer that way."

At first, he hesitated, then nodded his agreement. "Okay. But I'm with you."

"If you say so."

I briefed everyone and had the teams set their watches.

"We encircle the town and move in at four. Just before dawn."

"Why so late?" Larry asked.

"Because I said," I told him bluntly. "When you are the boss, you can set the time."

"What about the dawn?" one of the cartel people asked.

I stared at him. "It might save some of you shooting someone you're not meant to."

"I do not trust you, American."

"I don't give a fuck. Now, move out or you'll never move again. We go in at four."

They all disappeared into the dimness, leaving me and Larry. I looked at him. "You ready?"

He pulled what appeared to be a heavy-caliber handgun.

"What the fuck is that?"

"Colt Anaconda."

"You got a bugle too?" I asked him.

"What?"

"Never mind. Come on."

Heading off through the desert toward the lights of Retribution, we weaved between rocks and brush until we were within a stone's throw of the town. Taking cover in a dry wash, we observed the town for a few minutes. The lights we'd been able to see were streetlamps. I looked at my watch. It was just after three. It meant that all comms between Retribution and the outside world were down.

I scrambled back down into the bottom of the wash. Larry followed me. No sooner had I hit the sandy bottom than I turned, and my right hand struck out.

It was filled with a knife, the moonlight catching it as it flashed forward. The blade entered Larry's throat, and I used my strength to force it sideways.

It burst out of the other side in a spray of warm blood. I stepped back and watched as Larry staggered around on wobbly legs until they gave out. He slumped into the sand and arched his back before going still.

I wiped the blade on Larry's clothes and used some sand

to clean it better before putting it away. Then I climbed out of the dry wash and walked into Retribution.

"What was your plan at this point?" German asked me.

"I was going to warn the agents on site and start eliminating all threats."

"By eliminating, you mean kill?"

"Wasn't that rather risky?" Holland asked.

"They couldn't communicate with the outside world. As far as I was concerned, it was a contained environment."

Christine Ryan glanced at Newmann. "Did Mr. Kane come directly to you?"

"No, it was one of my men," the CIA director replied.

"What was Mr. Kane doing while that was happening?"

"Like he said, he was eliminating the threat."

I reached the first building and remained in the shadows. Glancing around, I tried to pick out any CIA operators. It looked clear, so I kept moving. With forty-five minutes remaining until kickoff, I had plenty of time to find someone to warn.

The town was in a far worse state than I remembered it being. Most of the stores were now closed, and the buildings damaged. From what I could see, a lot of the houses were vacant. Twenty minutes of furtive searching found me what I needed: a flicker of movement near a window.

It was an old store, once filled with goods and happy customers, now dust-filled and vacant except for rat droppings and the figure within. Moving to the alley behind the store, I crept in through the rear door. Trying to be as quiet as I could, I managed to find the CIA man's position. My handgun came up and I spoke quietly, "Don't turn around."

He froze. I could sense the tension in his body. "Who are you?"

"A friend."

"How do I know?"

"Do you have an earwig?"

"A what?"

He was stalling.

"Can Newman hear you?"

"Who?"

I took three quick strides across the room and put my handgun against the back of his head. "I don't have fucking time for this. Give me your earwig or I'll kill you and take it anyway."

He took it out and handed it over. Moments later, I said, "Newman, are you there? It's Kane."

"Kane? I'm going to kill you, you son of a bitch." No hello, what are you doing here? None of the social niceties you'd normally expect.

"Listen, we can deal with that later. Right now, there are a bunch of cartel shooters and bikers encircling the town about to move in. They think all comms are down. They obviously don't know about Oscar."

Oscar was the new encrypted system that the CIA was using for communications, which ran independent from all others. It was virtually impossible to jam and indestructible. Once losing regular comms, they would have switched over.

"What are you on about?" Newman growled.

"Listen. This whole thing is a trap to get you. I'll explain after, but right now, you need to be ready."

Sudden gunfire erupted from somewhere in the town. "Fuck, they're early. Newman, don't let anyone escape."

With Newman shouting over the comms, I gave the earwig back to the CIA operator. "I'd wait a moment before putting it back in."

Then I disappeared into the night.

There was widespread gunfire across the town now. A heated firefight where death or survival was the only result. Ahead of me, I made out a biker and a cartel shooter running across the dusty street. My AK-12 came up and I fired on the lead target. The cartel man stumbled and fell. The biker was too close to him and got tangled in his legs.

He too fell heavily and I waited for him to rise before firing. Dropping on top of the cartel shooter, he remained motionless.

I pushed along the street. To the east, daylight was throwing out its golden tendrils across the desert. Gunfire came from somewhere ahead of me. A single figure appeared, half running, half limping. He was followed by a biker.

The biker had a large caliber handgun in his fist and raised it to fire at the fleeing CIA man. My AK-12 began to speak once more. The biker staggered under the bullet strikes. But he was a big man and didn't fall. He turned to face me, a snarl of rage on his bearded face. I fired again, and this time, he died.

The running CIA operator stumbled and fell. I jogged over to him and crouched down. "Hey, are you alright?"

"Bastard shot me in the back. Who are you?"

"Come on, I'll get you into cover."

I helped him up and we moved into an alley. "Don't go anywhere."

He didn't respond.

A quick check confirmed what I had feared. I removed his earwig and jammed it into mine. It was alive with chatter. There were operators down everywhere. Over the top of it, I could hear Newman's steady voice trying to calm his people. Then an explosion could be heard, and things got worse.

———

The blast rocked the morning, seeming to shake Retribution to its disintegrating foundations. In turn, the explosion started a large fire, which began to spread quickly through the main street and across to the back blocks. Within twenty minutes, the town had gone from a war zone to an apocalypse.

"Newman, what was that?" I asked over the comms.

"Kane? What the fuck are you doing on this network?"

"What was the explosion?"

"A gas station in the center of town."

"How many people do you have left?"

"Enough," he replied.

"How many?" My voice was harsher this time, more insistent.

"I don't know."

"Shit, hang in there."

"I haven't forgotten what you did, Kane," he growled.

I said, "Hang on to that, Newman, and you might just get through this."

Moving out of the alley, I started pushing through town toward the old sheriff's office. It was derelict, all boarded over with used lumber and broken plywood. Ahead of me, the flames from the fire were leaping high into the air. I saw fleeting shadows. A running figure emerged from the conflagration, enveloped in fire. Another figure appeared. I heard the unmistakable deep-throated roar of a shotgun and the burning man folded over and fell to the street.

The AK in my hands came up and I sighted the biker. Three shots. At least one found its target. The biker died.

As I almost did.

A screaming figure came out of an alley to my right. One hand was holding a handgun, the other held a machete aloft. I think I recall his name was El Carnicero. He fired wildly at me, and I felt the passage of the bullets, one taking material and burning a furrow through the skin and flesh of my upper left arm.

The machete swung in a deadly arc, and I did the only thing I could. I let myself fall backward, dropping the AK and clawing for the handgun.

It came free of its holster and snapped into line. With a screech, the Mexican attempted to land another blow, but he'd have been better off just shooting me. The Glock in my hands opened up as I blasted six rounds into the killer's chest. The first three stopped him cold, the final three punched him backward, knocking him down hard. He sat there in shock, then his head came up and gave me a wicked grin. The Glock fired again, the back of his head blew out. There was no coming back from an injury like that.

I clenched my jaw, grinding my teeth against the burning pain emanating from the wound in my arm. There was blood leaking from the injury, but that was a problem for later. Right now, I had to find Newman.

"Newman?"

"What?"

"Where are you?"

My question was met with a long silence before he said, "Some joint called Reggie's."

The filing system in my mind ticked back and then I recalled the location. One street over from my position. "I'm coming to you."

"I'll be waiting."

I was acutely aware of the threat he'd made and the possibility that he might attempt to carry it out when I appeared.

The easiest way to get to Newman was through the main street. The issue was the apocalypse that stood between us. I figured if I kept to the center of the street, I would be fine.

The air was thick with acrid smoke, and the flames danced hungrily along the buildings, their orange tongues consuming the brittleness of the decayed wooden facades. The main street resembled a war zone. I stumbled over debris, my boots crunching on shattered glass and charred wood. The once-familiar street was a battleground where chaos reigned supreme.

My heart raced as I moved forward, the heat pressing against my skin like an invisible enemy. The storefronts that had once displayed their wares were now twisted, blackened skeletons. Their windows shattered, the shards glinting like malevolent eyes. The scent of burning paint and melting plastic filled my nostrils, choking me.

I glanced left and right, my gaze catching glimpses of

movement within the inferno. Shadows darted behind broken windows, figures desperate to escape the relentless flames. But there was no salvation here—only the unceasing march of destruction. I wondered how many lives were trapped within those crumbling walls, their screams swallowed by the roar of the fire.

The asphalt bubbled, sticky, clawing at my boots. I pressed forward, my breath ragged, my eyes stinging from the smoke. The flames seemed to mock me, dancing higher, their crackling laughter echoing in my ears.

And then, as if in response to my defiance, the ground trembled. A building collapsed, sending a plume of ash and sparks into the sky like a cluster of fireworks. I staggered, shielding my face, my heart pounding. The world around me blurred—a nightmare of heat and destruction.

But I couldn't stop. I wouldn't stop. My legs carried me onward, driven by a desperate need to survive. The fire consumed everything—the memories, the laughter, the mundane routines of life. It was a cleansing force, ruthless and indiscriminate.

As I reached the end of the street, I turned back for one last look. The flames had devoured links to my past, leaving only charred remnants.

Relief was short-lived as several figures emerged from the black smoke. Two men, one cartel, the other a biker, were dragging a CIA operator. He was bloody and looked to be unconscious. "What the fuck are you doing?" I demanded.

"Keeping the prick for later so we can have some fun," the biker growled.

"We don't have time for that shit," I snarled and lifted my AK, squeezing the trigger.

Two short bursts saw the two would-be torturers drop dead with bullets in them. I bent down and checked the CIA operator and found a pulse. "Shit."

I couldn't abandon him to die at the hands of the enemy, so I leaned down and lifted him over my shoulder. He groaned in response, but I kept moving.

An explosion detonated from somewhere behind me. I guessed a propane tank had succumbed to the heat. The fireball rose skyward in a mushroom cloud. Up ahead, I saw the alley I needed to take to get me across to Reggie's.

About to turn into the mouth of the alley, I saw a cartel shooter ahead of me. He was covered in blood, and I seriously doubted that it was his. My Glock came up as he saw me and hesitated. His head, just above his eyeline, bore the brunt of my shot. It snapped back violently, and he fell to the ground.

Stepping over his supine figure, our journey continued. I paused at the gaping alley mouth, where a quick glance left and right told me that it was clear. It was here I realized something. The gunfire had dropped considerably. Adjusting the man on my shoulders, I headed through the dusty and weed-choked alley to the far end. Peering around the corner into the daylight-filled street, I saw Reggie's farther along on the right.

Making a decision about the unconscious man on my back, I walked up to the open front door and almost walked into a bullet.

The round gouged out a chunk of wood from the doorframe near my head. I lurched back, the weight on my shoulder suddenly heavy as fuck. A voice came from within. "Did I get you, you son of a bitch?"

"Newman? What the fuck are you doing? I've already been shot once this morning. I don't plan on it again."

"I told you I'd kill you for what you did. You got her killed."

"Elana?" I was surprised at his commitment to an officer. "Why? Not like a director to get personally attached to his field agents."

"She was my niece, you fuck."

"Christ, I don't have time for this, Newman. Just listen. I'm coming in. If you try to shoot me again, I will react."

Drawing a deep breath, I crossed the threshold and entered Reggie's. He was in the front of the store. The early morning light was starting to filter inside as the sun rose above the desert.

"Who is that?" he asked.

"No idea. He's one of yours."

Newman nodded abruptly. "Put him down over there and start explaining."

He maintained the grip on his handgun, and I could see the inner turmoil as he wrestled with his desire to kill me.

I said, "You know I'm in Cuba to destroy the missiles. I've managed to make a start, but Morozov had them moved. Now I'm trying to locate them again."

"In Retribution?"

"I managed to get inside. Convince him I've changed sides. But he wants further confirmation."

"How?"

"I have to take him your head."

Newman's face remained passive. "You might have a problem with that."

"It's a problem I'm working on. First, we need to finish off the rest of the cartel killers and the bikers. I have an idea about the rest of it."

"And my niece? Was she just collateral damage, or your way in?"

I was about to reply when the sound of close gunfire shattered the early morning. I rolled away as bullets sprayed the interior of the store. A cry of pain from Newman told me he was hit. I came up with my Glock clear and fired at the assailant in the doorway. Both shots hit home, and the would-be killer sank to his knees.

I fired again and he fell onto his side.

Newman was hit, but not mortally. I checked him over to find it was a graze along his side. He cursed me while I was doing it, and when I was finished, I stood and said, "Wait here."

"Where are you going?"

"I've still got things to do."

It took me another thirty minutes of searching to find the

bikers as well as the rest of the cartel men who had come from Cuba with me. There were three—none by the time I was done. When I went back to Reggie's, Newman was still awake and coherent. "Everything is fine now," I informed him. "They're all dead."

The CIA director glared at me. "What now?"

"I need your head."

"He obviously didn't take it," Holland said, interrupting.

It was a stupid statement from an equally stupid man. I was starting to wonder why he was even on the panel. "Obviously."

"You left quite a mess in Retribution, Mr. Kane," German said.

I nodded. "Twenty-four dead. Not all my doing."

"And how did you cover it up, exactly?" Christine Ryan asked.

Newman cleared his throat. "The FBI declared that all the deceased had died in the explosion and subsequent fire. They were able to tidy it up and sit on it."

Christine Ryan stared at me. "And you, Mr. Kane. What did you do?"

"I took Morozov his head."

CHAPTER 12

MOROZOV WAS HOLED UP IN A RENOVATED PLANTATION HOUSE surrounded by bodyguards and Igoshin's people. Kokorin had departed while I was in the US. I'd flown into a small airstrip from Mexico. That had been eventful in itself.

Garcia had called in a favor from someone within the Mexican cartel. It was organized that I was to overnight in Mexico City and then fly from there. Things started out fine. I was put up in a hotel with a pool and restaurant downstairs. That evening, I headed for dinner and was at the bar having a drink when I was approached by a woman. One look was all it took to notice the black dress, split to the hip on one side, exposing a great leg. Her long dark hair fell in waves across flawless bronze skin, her dark eyes accentuated perfectly by a touch of makeup and expertly shaped eyebrows. You might say, a tall drink of cool water.

She sat beside me and said, "Buy me a drink, American."

Looking around the restaurant, I said, "Why would I do that?"

"Because I am thirsty, and you are curious."

I swept the room again.

"Do not worry, I am here alone."

"That's what worries me." I waved at the bartender. "I'll have a whiskey and get the lady a…"

"Tequila," she replied.

I nodded. "Tequila."

The bartender nodded and the woman said, "I am Manuela."

"John."

"Why are you in Mexico City, John?"

"Just passing through," I replied.

"Oh?"

"To Cuba."

"Business?"

"Yes. What about you?"

"Business and pleasure," Manuela informed me.

"Not from Mexico?"

"Spain."

I stared at her alluring eyes. The woman was dangerous.

Manuela said, "Will you dine with me, John?"

What was it they said? Keep your friends close and your enemies closer? "Sure."

After the bartender presented our drinks, we downed them before turning to look for a table. Finding one in a secluded corner, we sat down and then waited as a hostess came with menus. Ordering a bottle of champagne, we began to study the menu. Looking over at Manuela, I asked, "What do you desire?"

"Oysters." The tip of her tongue touched her top lip, leaving a glistening trail on the dark gray lipstick. "What do you think?"

Her question was to gauge my interest in sharing them with her. "Sure. Why not?"

We engaged in small talk while awaiting our meal, Manuela flirting outrageously. Once the oysters were gone, we took what remained of the bottle of champagne and went back to my room, where we indulged in a few rounds of night maneuvers.

Nothing happened.

It wasn't until around three in the morning when things went pear-shaped. Two figures were trying to gain access to the room using a door key. I wasn't aware of their presence until Manuela clamped a slim-fingered hand over my mouth and whispered into my ear. "Someone is outside."

I listened and heard the door go. We lay still, eyes open, watching the intruders come toward the bed. Before I could respond, Manuela was up and running, the empty champagne bottle in her hand.

Her movements could be described as a graceful ballet of death, which took me completely by surprise even though I was already wary of her.

The bottle took the weapon of the first shooter and shattered. The suppressed handgun flew across the room and thudded onto the carpeted floor. Still moving in her deadly dance, Manuela swept the broken bottle around and drove the jagged edges into the second killer's throat. She pushed it savagely, the sharp edges tearing through flesh in a spray of hot blood.

The killer grasped at the ghastly wound and staggered back. However, Manuela wasn't done. She turned back to the first intruder who lunged toward her. Still holding the bloody, broken bottle, her hand drove forward. Straight and true.

Replicating her movements, the killer fell beside his friend, where they died in an expanding pool of combined blood.

Manuela stopped moving, poised like a cat. She wasn't even breathing heavily. I flicked on the light and saw what resembled a slaughterhouse floor rather than a hotel room. Manuela's naked form was slick with blood. She looked at herself in the mirror. "I need a shower."

She disappeared into the bathroom. I heard the shower start a few moments later. Both dead men were covered in tattoos. They were obviously Cartel.

Five minutes later, when Manuela reappeared, tousling her hair with a towel, I stared at her. "Who are you?"

She hesitated before saying, "Holly sent me to find you."

I shook my head. "No, that's not what I meant."

"GROM."

She was Polish counter-terror. "Why has Holly got you out here?"

"After what happened to you and the report she got from the SAS team, she decided to send me with my special talents."

I glanced at the bodies once more. "They are definitely a worthy skill set."

Ten minutes later, Manuela was dressed and gone.

I left the hotel, and twelve hours later, I was back in Cuba. Which brings me back to the—

"Wait," German said and turned his attention to Holly. "You had Polish Special forces sent to Mexico to find Mr. Kane?"

Holly shook her head. "No, to Arizona. She picked up his trail there. Followed him to Mexico City."

"So much for a British-only operation."

"I utilized every asset I could lay my hands on. This operation wasn't contained. It was global. I did what I deemed necessary to accomplish a result. You see, Poland was under direct threat if Russia rolled across the frontier. They were all too willing to assist."

"Wait, before we go any further, what happened to Maria, the young woman you gave up to Morozov?" Christine Ryan asked.

"The SAS team intercepted her transport and extracted her. She currently resides in Oxfordshire, where she has a job working in a village store under an assumed name."

"What name would that be?" Holland asked.

My eyes narrowed. "The common name of none of your fucking business."

He opened his mouth to speak when Christine Ryan cut him off. "Let's continue, gentlemen. The afternoon is wearing on and we still have a lot to cover."

When I went to see Morozov, I was carrying a cooler. Entering the room, I placed it on the desk before him and stepped back. He looked at me and then at Igoshin before coming back to me. "What is this?"

"You said you wanted his head?"

Morozov looked at the container and then said, "What happened?"

"It was a shit fight from the start. One of the cartel guys was seen before we could get into place. Then one of the bikers blew the fucking shit out of a propane tank and shit went to something a lot fucking worse."

Igoshin stared at me. The skepticism on his face lay bare. "It seems convenient that you are the only one to escape."

"That's because I'm the only one who knew what I was doing," I replied. "Sending those bastards with me. It would have been better if some of Grigori's people had come. At least they have military training."

Igoshin muttered something under his breath and walked to the desk. Without hesitation, he opened the cooler, revealing the blackened, bloody head with almost all of the flesh on it charred away. He looked up at me and said, "This could be anyone."

Morozov nodded. "It indeed could be. How do I know that this is CIA Director Newman?"

"You'll just have to take my word for it."

The Russian general shook his head. He closed the lid. "No. Unless you can prove that it is him, then I cannot trust you. And if I cannot trust you, then I have no alternative but to hand you over to Julio."

"Get it tested," I said. "The blood is still fresh enough. You should be able to get results from that."

"Maybe I will do that. Now, another problem. It would seem that our little bird has flown with help. The Cubans are looking for them, but perhaps you might shed some light on where they have gone?"

I stared at him, barely contained relief coursing through my body, but I remained stoic. "When?"

"The day you left."

"Then you won't find them. They will be gone."

"You sound certain."

"I am."

Morozov nodded slowly. "Very well. Leave us."

I stood there unmoved.

"Is there a problem?"

"And go where?"

"Anywhere in Cuba. Grigori will give you a cell phone. When it rings, answer it. If you don't, I will send people to kill you."

"What if I accidentally miss a call?" I asked the Russian.

"Don't."

I left the office accompanied by Igoshin. Once outside, he turned on me and said, "You are a man not to be trusted, Kane. I know you are up to something, and I will find out. When I do, I will skin you slowly, roll you in a salt bin, and start again."

My stare remained fixed on the mercenary's. "You won't have to, Grigory, because if I'm up to something, you are the one I will kill first. Now, where is that cell?"

———

I was sitting in a café, drinking coffee, when Manuela next appeared. I'd been back in Cuba for a day and was trying to plan my next move. It was futile attempting to contact the SAS team because I was almost certainly being watched and didn't know if they were still in the country. I had no idea where they were.

"Buy a girl a coffee?"

Looking up, I saw her standing there. "You are taking a risk."

"Which is why I am dressed the way I am," she replied.

Her short red dress was open down the front, revealing more than a hint of breast and lacy undergarment. "You look like a prostitute."

"Which is exactly the look I was going for."

I nodded to the seat across from me. Manuela sat down and said, "There is a man at the table near the front door."

"My tail?" I asked.

"Yes. He is Russian. Someone doesn't trust you."

"What are you doing here?" I asked her.

"Making contact. Your friends are holed up outside of Havana. The package they extracted is on its way to the UK."

"That's something, I guess."

"What is your next move?"

"I need to get in contact with the team," I said.

"That's why I'm here," Manuela said as she reached out and took my hand.

"Where are they?" I asked her.

"Holed up in a safe place outside the city."

"I need you tonight," I told her.

"Oh, baby," she replied with a grin.

"Not like that. I'm going after Garcia."

Her smile widened. "Are you sure that is wise?"

"If I can take him off the board, it will free me up to concentrate on Morozov and the missiles."

"Why not just take him?"

"Because he'll give me nothing. He'd rather die. I know. Can you help me?"

"Of course. What do you want me to tell Cramer?"

"Tell him to sit tight. Reach out to Holly and see if we can get access to a satellite tonight. Cramer can run ISR from where he's based."

"Okay, I'll do what I can."

"Nothing about the missiles from their end?"

"No."

"Where the hell can they be hiding them?"

"I don't know, sweetie." She stood up, walked around the table, and leaned down to kiss me. "I'll see you tonight."

"You don't even know where," I whispered.

"Yes, I do."

And then she was gone.

A few minutes later, I stood up and walked toward the door. As I passed my shadow, I bumped into his table, spilling his drink. "Sorry, pal."

———

Taking a risk that could cost me my life, I left the cell provided by Morozov in my hotel room. Going over the balcony, I climbed down into the lush garden below. From there, I headed out onto the street, where I found Manuela waiting in a dark blue van. She saw me and flashed the lights. I ran over to the vehicle and climbed in.

"Do you know where to go?" I asked.

"Of course."

She drove through the streets, taking us to a part of the city where the larger colonials with spacious gardens were situated. Pulling over and parking deep in the shadows of a darkened street, we climbed out. Heading to open the back door, I found everything we needed for the mission there. An AK-12, body armor, night vision, a black jumpsuit, and a mask. Manuela passed me a small container. I opened it and found an earwig. I put it in and said, "Cramer, copy?"

"Copy, Kane."

"How are we looking?"

"We're good to go. We have a bird in the air, and we can see for four blocks. Looks like there are eight X-rays on the ground and a couple inside."

"Any sign of Garcia?"

"Negative."

"We just have to assume he is there," I replied.

Cramer said, "When you get into place, let me know. I'll cut the power for that location."

"That would be great."

"Just say when. By the way, that's some friend you have there."

"Thank you," Manuela said.

We moved into position and crouched in the shadows. I said into my comms, "Cramer, do it."

"Roger that. Here comes the night."

A heartbeat later, the power was cut, and everything was dark. "You ready?"

Manuela pulled down her NVGs. "Let's do this."

We scaled the chest-high stone wall and dropped into a crouch on the other side. I scanned the scene before me. A large expanse of lawn, shrubs, garden beds, and the obligatory pool and paved area.

"At your ten, Reaper," Cramer said in a calm voice.

The suppressed AK came up and around. My finger stroked the trigger, and I felt the recoil against my shoulder. The bullets struck with an audible thunk, and the cartel soldier dropped to the damp grass.

Moving forward, I was not concerned about hiding the body. There wasn't time. A flashlight appeared to my right. Behind me, Manuela's weapon came to life and death touched another cartel killer.

We never broke stride. The garden bed ahead of me proved no obstacle as I walked straight through it. "Reaper, hold."

Going to our knees, we waited in silence, watching for any movement. Ahead of me, I saw two more flashlights appear. "Take the one on the left," I whispered to Manuela.

"Copy."

Moments later, on my cue, we fired, and the two men died. "X-rays down. We're Charlie Mike."

Pressing forward toward the patio and the pool area, we heard, "Two o'clock."

Another guard died on the hard paved area with a few rounds in his chest. Continuing our steady progress around the pool, we stopped before the French doors. Reaching out, I touched the handle, which turned easily, and the door opened.

In my ear, Cramer said, "There are two people inside the building, Reaper. One is toward the front of the house, the other upstairs in one of the bedrooms."

"Copy."

I let the AK hang by its strap and drew my suppressed Glock. My path led me toward the downstairs target at the front of the house. They were in the living room. We entered and the person leaped to their feet. The target was armed, so I shot them. Flicking on my small flashlight to identify the body, I concluded that it wasn't Garcia.

Using hand signals, I indicated upstairs. Manuela nodded and fell in behind me. I started up and had just lowered my foot on the second step when Cramer said, "Target on the move. Coming your way."

I paused, holding up my left fist, making sure Manuela saw it. We waited. My Glock pointed up the staggered incline. The figure appeared. My finger twitched but I held my fire. It was a woman. Slim, dressed in a nightgown, unarmed. Then, with the aid of the ambient light, she saw us standing there. And screamed.

"He's not here," I said. "We need to leave."

With the screams ringing in our ears, we backed away from the stairs and headed for the exit, retracing our steps.

Once outside, Cramer gave me a warning. A figure was running in from our left. I swung the AK around and opened fire. His momentum carried him forward, and he face-planted on the sandstone pavers.

From then on, we ran. Bullets and shouts chased us toward the perimeter. We leaped over the stone wall, and I heard the distinct sounds of rounds crashing into the obstacle.

Moments later, we were in the van and rocketing away from Garcia's home.

"Reaper, there are warnings and alarms going out city-wide. You need to get the fuck back to the hotel now."

"Doing our best," I replied.

Manuela seemed to have a built-in GPS and knew when to turn. She made all the correct moves like a precision driver should, and before I knew what was happening, we had returned to the spot just one block from the hotel.

"Reaper, Grigori Igoshin has just turned up at your hotel with a crew. You need to shift your ass."

"Working on it," I replied.

We ran as fast as we could to the hotel. As we went, I said, "You don't need to do this."

"It will help."

Reaching the hotel, we started the climb to my room. On the way up, I heard Cramer say, "They're about to get out of the elevator."

This was cutting it close. Then, as I grabbed the rail for my own balcony, I knew we weren't going to make it.

"Fuck," I growled in defeat.

"Wait," Manuela said hurriedly. "Take off your clothes."

"What?"

"Do it." As I started to peel my shirt off, she was almost naked. "Everything. Take it all off."

Moments later, I was naked, and my clothes were tossed with hers in the darkened recess of the balcony. Without any time to spare, Manuela leaped at me, wrapping her legs around my back, and kissed me. It was at that moment that the room door crashed back and Igoshin and his people erupted into my room.

On cue, Manuela started to scream in ecstasy.

"What the fuck are you doing here, Igoshin?" I shouted at him. Manuela clung to me, her cries silenced. "Can't you see I'm busy?"

"Who is she?" he snarled.

"Mind your own fucking business."

He glared at us both and then snarled loudly before turning and storming out. Manuela started to giggle. I said, "What's so fucking funny? That was close."

"I was just thinking that you were under so much stress and yet you still got an erection."

"Shit, it was a bit hard not to."

"Well?"

"Well, what?"

"Are you going to let it go to waste?"

It was my turn to laugh. "I don't think so."

CHAPTER 13

THE FOLLOWING DAY, I FLICKED ON THE TELEVISION AND SAW that things were hotting up in Europe. Russia, or the USSR as it was now known again, had mobilized its troops into Belarus. Reports were that 300,000 frontline fighters had been assembled, along with tanks and other mechanized units. From the Kremlin, Sergey Lash was beating the drums of war against NATO, condemning the west's encroachment of the mother country's borders and their influence in destabilizing the countries around him.

It was the start of the Russian plan. It was coinciding with the elections in the UK which were to be held soon. But that was the plan. They also had other contingencies in place, but you will hear about them tomorrow.

I turned the television off and walked out to the balcony I'd used the night before. Manuela had gone and I was now alone.

Morozov chose that moment to pay me a visit. The door was still busted from Igoshin's little foray. And speak of the devil, he was right there with him.

"Good morning, John," Morozov said as he walked in.

"Gennady. What do I owe the pleasure of this visit?"

"I thought you might like to come for a drive with me," he replied.

"Is there any use in saying no?"

He shrugged. "Not really."

"So, is this a one-way ticket?" I asked him.

Morozov shook his head. "No, no. I had the blood on the head analyzed. It came back positive."

German cleared his throat, causing me to stop. "Did they have Director Newman's blood on file?"

I opened my mouth to speak but Newman beat me to it. "No, they had a mole on the inside. We'd suspected it for a while, but once things started to happen, the mole's activity picked up."

"I'm curious," Christine Ryan said. "Whose head was it?"

"One of the bikers," I replied. "I cut it off and threw it in the fire for a while."

She pulled a face. "Such a barbaric act. And the blood?"

"The CIA guys had field medical kits. I drew some blood from the director and put it on the head. What remained of it, anyway. And before you say anything, I needed to do it to gain his trust. Plus, Director Newman had an obituary put in the Washington Post and went into hiding while I was still with Morozov."

"Why didn't the director just blow your story out of the water, Mr. Kane?" Holland asked. "He was angry enough with you to do it."

"Because they were the bigger threat. Especially to the US."

"Continue," German said.

Morozov held up a newspaper he'd brought with him. "This helps confirm it."

He passed the paper over to me. It was a copy of the Washington Post.

"Go to the obituaries, John. You will find it."

I flicked through the paper and found what I knew to be there. It was an obituary for Newman. "Is that proof enough for you?"

"I still cannot understand why you are doing this?" Morozov said.

"Money," I replied. "I help, and you pay me well."

"What makes you think I need you?"

"You've seen what I can do. If you don't want me, Shatov will."

"Something tells me not to trust you, John, but I have conferred with Mikhail, and for some reason, he does. So, let's go."

We went downstairs and climbed into a solid Humvee. Igoshin drove us out of the city and into the jungle. "I see Lash has massed troops along the Polish border."

"Along with the Baltic fleet," Morozov said.

"What, you plan on invading Poland? Is that it?"

Morozov smiled. "Sometimes things may not be as they seem."

"So Poland isn't your target?"

He smiled at me once more, and we drove on.

The journey took a turn from the familiar to the unexpected as we veered off the sealed road, leaving behind the smoothness of asphalt for the road noise of gravel beneath our tires. For an hour, we were flanked by dense jungle. Then, as if stepping through a portal, we left the embrace of the jungle and entered an open clearing. It was not grand in size, but it was significant in its contents—a missile launcher stood there, imposing and unexpected. It was as if the jungle had kept this secret, revealing it only to those who dared to journey through its depths.

The vehicle came to a halt on the rough terrain, its engine quieting to a soft purr before silence took over. We disembarked, our boots crunching on the gravel beneath us. I made my way toward the missile, its metallic surface gleaming ominously under the harsh glare of the Cuban sun. As I stood there, a sense of helplessness washed over me. I wished fervently for a charge, something powerful enough to neutralize the threat that loomed before us.

"Comrade General!"

I turned and saw Sepp Kahn, the scientist, hurrying toward Morozov. "What is it, Sepp?"

"We have a problem."

"What problem?" Morozov's voice had taken on a deathly tone.

"The missiles do not have enough range. The new engines have a fault."

"What? Why are we only finding this out now?"

"I discovered it by accident. They need to be placed closer," Khan informed him.

"How much closer?" Morozov asked.

Kahn muttered something under his breath, the words so soft and fleeting that they were lost to me. His eyes never met mine, and I wondered if he even registered that I was there. His fingers fidgeted, a clear sign of his nervousness. He was like a bird caught in a snare. All his usual bravado evaporated, leaving him timid and unsure. His gaze was fixed on Morozov, who was deep in thought, oblivious to Kahn's growing anxiety. Kahn's shoulders were hunched, his entire body seemed to be wound tighter than a spring, a physical sign of his inner turmoil as he waited, almost too patiently, for Morozov to unravel the knot of his problem.

"All of them, Sepp?"

"Yes, Comrade General."

More words were spoken, but I could only make out one. Matanzas.

Kahn hurried away and I walked over to Morozov. "Problems?"

"Nothing that can't be fixed."

I was about to ask more questions when Igoshin came over to us with a tablet in his hands. He wasn't alone. Three of his people came with him.

"It seems we have another issue, General."

Morozov sighed. "It would be the day for it."

"Last night you know of the issue at Julio's home?"

"Yes, yes."

"I took a team to check on our new friend. When we entered his room, he was found in a compromising position with this woman."

Morozov took the screen and then passed it over to me. I

looked down at it and saw Manuela staring back at me. She was fully clothed, of course, but instead of wearing civilian clothes, she was dressed in the uniform of a GROM officer.

I looked up at Morozov. "Well, that's shit."

"And immediately, we go back to the point where I cannot trust you. Grigori, take him to Julio. Let him deal with it."

"Yes, General."

"And find the woman. I want to know what she does."

————

Julio Garcia seemed overjoyed to see me. His grin was broad, and his teeth gleamed white as he stared at me. "This is going to be a great honor to have you as my guest."

He found refuge at a secluded horse stud, nestled away from the city's relentless pace. It was a pastoral haven where green paddocks rolled like emerald carpets, separated by pristine white fences that gleamed under the sun's touch. The heart of the estate was a grand brick stable, its architecture boasting a 30-horse capacity.

I guess Garcia had to spend his billions on something.

Beyond the stable's sturdy confines, the horse pool lay like a mirror reflecting the sky's mood. It was a luxurious aquatic retreat for the horses, designed to provide relief from the heat and to aid in their recovery and training. The water rippled as the horses enjoyed its cool embrace.

This stud was a world unto itself, a place where the city's distant hum was replaced by the serene sounds of nature and the cries of the tortured.

"Don't get too attached," I told him. "I don't plan on being around too long."

"Something we agree on," Garcia stated. "Was it you who came to my home in Havana last night?"

"I was in bed."

Garcia shrugged. "I guess we will find out eventually."

"I suppose you couldn't just take my word for it?"

The look he gave me was contemptuous.

I shrugged. "I guess not."

"Take him and put him in one of the stables. I will deal with him later."

In the dimly lit stable, they led me past the rows of occupied stalls, their inhabitants snorting and shifting restlessly. The air was thick with the scent of hay and horse, a pungent reminder of where I found myself. They stopped at an unoccupied stall, its door hanging open like a silent invitation to a darker fate. With rough hands, they pushed me inside, the straw-covered floor scratchy against my skin.

The stall was humid, the air stale and heavy. Producing an iron dog collar, its cold metal surface gleaming faintly in the low light, they fastened it around my neck, its weight a tangible symbol of my captivity. The collar was attached to a heavy chain, which they secured to the wall, the clinking sound echoing ominously in the confined space.

Chained up, I could only watch as they retreated, the sound of their footsteps fading until I was left in silence. The reality of my situation settled in, the collar a constant, uncomfortable presence. It was a harsh reminder of my vulnerability, the iron band a barrier to any thoughts of escape. In that empty stall, with only the occasional shuffle and snort of the horses nearby, I was left to contemplate the uncertain future that awaited me.

As the sun began its descent, painting the sky in hues of orange and pink, Garcia came to the stable, flanked by three of his most trusted men. The air was filled with a sense of expectancy, punctuated by the distant murmur of voices that grew steadily in volume and clarity.

The door to the stall opened and Garcia entered. One of his men was carrying a chair. He and two others dragged me out into the main stable and forced me to sit on it.

Garcia stared at me. "So, the time has come. Do you have anything to say?"

"Would it matter if I did?"

"Not really."

"Then fuck you."

He hit me and I fell off the seat.

"Get him up," Garcia snarled. "Get the drill."

Sitting me back up, they made sure I was fixed firmly to the seat. Then one of Garcia's men stood in front of me, holding a battery-powered drill. He stroked the trigger and it whirred to life.

"Are you sure you have a big enough bit?" I asked.

Garcia took it from his man and proceeded to drill a hole in my thigh. I screamed. I couldn't help it. I'd been beaten and waterboarded, but the tearing, burning pain elicited by the drill bit was like nothing I had ever felt before. And it wasn't even that big.

Garcia stepped back and smiled. It was a cold, malevolent smile brought about by the ecstasy of inflicting pain. My cheeks puffed out with every breath I drew into my lungs as I fought back the last vestiges of pain. Through gritted teeth, I grated, "Incestuous motherfucker."

So, he put another hole in my leg next to the first, and I screamed again. Pulling the bit from my muscle, he held it aloft for me to see. There was flesh still clinging to the metal, and blood dripped to the ground.

"Now, what have you got to tell me?"

"Fuck you." My voice was becoming hoarse.

It was the answer Garcia seemed to be hoping for. Reaching into his pocket, he retrieved another drill bit. This one was at least a quarter inch thick, capable of doing far more damage.

"What do you think about this one?"

"I'd prefer that you stick it up your ass," I replied.

"How about I use it on yours?"

Sometimes, it pays to keep your mouth shut.

Garcia nodded at one of his men, and before I knew what

was happening, he'd hit me, knocking me senseless. While I was stunned, they untied me and forced me face-down over the seat, ripping my jeans down and exposing my ass.

While this was happening, Garcia was relishing the act of changing the drill bit. I fought against it with all the strength I could muster, but the effects of the blow I'd received still had me rattled. Garcia stepped closer, the whirr of the drill affecting my mind.

Garcia said, "Enjoy, Mr. Kane."

My body tensed, muscles bunched in preparation against the excruciating pain that was about to assault not only my body but my senses as well. My mind willed me to fight, and just as I was about to launch into a frenzy, one of the body-guards' heads snapped back, his brains blowing out through a hole punched in his skull by a 5.56 round.

Garcia screamed in frustration as he dropped the drill and started to run. His remaining two bodyguards released me and went for their weapons. More rounds ripped through the stable, and the two remaining cartel men dropped to the floor, bleeding out from multiple bullet wounds.

"Get him up," I heard Cramer say.

I felt rough hands dragging me to my feet. "Easy, chaps," I said, grabbing my pants, pulling them up.

"Can you walk, Kane?" Ted asked.

"I might need some help," I allowed. "The bastard drilled my leg."

"That's all right, mate, lean on me."

All I can say is it was a good thing he was as big as me. Leaving the stable, we headed for a horse paddock. Hooky was on point, and I heard Cramer say, "Overwatch is saying we need to fucking move."

Suddenly, the crack of a sniper rifle reached out across the paddock, followed by another one. "Who's that," I asked Ted, because I knew all the Brits were with me.

"That's your girlfriend, mate," Ted replied. "She's a tough cow that one."

"I wouldn't let her hear you say that," I grunted.

"You're right."

Behind us, I heard the suppressed rattle of Shorty's weapon, followed by Cramer's call: "Keep pushing, keep pushing."

The dew on the ground was a carpet of silvery droplets cast by the Cuban moon. The cool night air was a welcome relief after the humid stable I'd been chained to. Hobbling as fast as I could, the residual pain from my wounds reminded me they hadn't gone anywhere, every step. However, I was more of a hindrance to Ted than anything else. Bullets from the pursuing Mexicans were chasing us hard across the open ground.

"Fuck it. Ted, let me go, I'll manage."

"You sure, mate?"

"Yes, do it."

As soon as he released my weight, I stumbled like a drunk coming off a Saturday night bender before gathering myself and straightening. "Are you alright?" Ted asked me.

"Fine, give me a weapon."

Pulling his handgun, he handed it to me. "It's good to go, Reaper. Point and shoot."

"Thanks." Then I started what could be only classed as hobble running.

"Keep going straight ahead," Ted called across to me.

The intensity of my pain would have debilitated a weaker person, but I'd learned to compartmentalize over the years, and after a while, I felt it fade to a nagging throb.

When I made the edge of the jungle, the undergrowth swallowed me. A short time later, I was joined by the SAS operators, my rescuers.

Cramer asked, "You okay, Reaper?"

"I'll live."

Leaves and branches began raining down around us, marking the passage of the incoming rounds that were decimating the vegetation.

"Come on," Ted said to me.

Then I heard Cramer say, "Vixen One, move to the RV."

Keeping up our forward momentum through the jungle, the gunfire eventually stopped, and all sounds of pursuit died away. After walking for what felt like days, we made it to the RV point to find Manuela already waiting for us. "It is good to see you alive, John."

"It's good to be alive," I replied and grabbed a canteen of water from one of the men.

"You want to tell us about it?" Cramer asked.

"How about when we get back," I said, taking several gulps of cool water. "Wherever that is."

"All right, Shorty, lead out."

Our journey recommenced, following Shorty through the jungle, the nagging pain in my leg becoming harder to ignore.

CHAPTER 14

BASE CAMP CAME IN THE FORM OF AN OLD RUNDOWN COLONIAL slowly being reclaimed by the jungle. The undergrowth was thick all around it and the place was in serious need of a facelift, and a gardener. Once we arrived back, I fell into a chair while Ted began tending my wounds, cleaning the blood from my leg that had seeped through my pants during the hike. He set up an IV line and put an antibiotic into the bag. To make sure, he hit me with a syringe of the stuff as well. "No telling what manner of shit was on that bit, Reaper. Better doing this than having you medevacked to get your leg amputated."

Next, he injected a local anesthetic around the wound site and started to clean the holes. When he was done, he said, "I'll replace the dressing tomorrow. We need to keep it clean. There is a good possibility that it will have some infection, but I'm hoping we can kill it quickly."

"How much of that local do you have?"

"Not a lot."

"Save some for me. I might need it."

Cramer poked his head in. "You ready for debrief, Reaper?"

"Yeah, let's get it done. While it's still fresh in my head."

We gathered in what had been the colonial's drawing

room. Manuela and Shorty were working at a laptop, deep in discussion, but looked up when Cramer said, "Gather around."

Everyone moved in and sat or stood closer, giving their full attention. I caught sight of Manuela, who smiled at me. I sighed, suddenly exhausted, not only physically, but mentally.

"Okay. From what I can gather, there is something wrong with the rocket motors on the missiles. They mentioned something about Matanzas."

"Matanzas, as in the town?" Hooky asked.

"Sounds like it."

"Why Matanzas?" Cramer asked.

"Something to do with distance."

"What else?"

I said, "You tell me. What have I missed?"

Cramer said, "Troops mobilized in Belarus and bombs going off in Helsinki and London."

"Helsinki?"

"Yes, the government there has been outspoken against the Lash government. The Russians have moved troops to the border there in an act of intimidation."

"Are they going to cross?"

"Don't know, but with the British elections not far away, Pridham is urging more focus on home security and less on Europe. Secure your own backyard first. And they're buying it."

"That's what they want," I said.

"You mean the Russians?" Manuela asked.

"Yes. The Generals and Lash. It's part of their plan. They want everyone looking elsewhere."

"You think they put the bombs in London?" Cramer asked.

I nodded. "Wars swing elections. After coming out of Afghanistan, the last thing the British public want is to get involved in another war. That is what Pridham is counting on."

"You make him sound like a Russian plant," Ted said.

"That's what Knocker and Holly are trying to find out. We think he is Dolos. Greek for the God of Trickery. These missiles are designed to keep the US out. The question is, where are they?"

Shorty said, "We have a satellite, I'll have a look around Matanzas."

"We need to find Morozov again, as well as Kahn, the scientist."

Cramer nodded. "And Garcia."

I nodded and grunted, "And Garcia."

———

"I can find nothing around Matanzas," Shorty told me. "There is no sign of Morozov nor of the scientist."

"What about Garcia?" I asked.

"He's the only prick we could find," Shorty said. He laid out a map on a rickety table. It had been two days since I'd been pulled out of Garcia's stables, and the wounds in my leg were healing well. The map was of Havana. "Garcia is holed up here. British intelligence are ninety percent sure."

He was pointing at an apartment block in what looked to be the slum area. "There."

I stared at the map. "Do we have photos?"

"Yes." Picking up his tablet, he opened a file then passed it across to me and said, "In the middle of hell."

It looked like the middle of Aleppo while sustaining heavy bombing. "What happened here?" I asked.

"Earthquake years ago. In the early days, when the Cubans first started building with concrete, there were no codes. The first big earthquake came along and fucked the whole area up. The place came down like a deck of cards."

"How big an area?"

"Five, six blocks."

"The streets look reasonably clear," I pointed out.

"Yes, but it's a fucking prick of a place to assault. That's why the police stay out of there. The ones who aren't corrupt, anyway."

"What's so special about it?" I asked.

"It's where he keeps most of his drugs and money. Similar to a bank. It is all stored underground," Shorty said.

"Basement?" I asked.

"Yeah, a whole network just like Aleppo."

"So, he's in there somewhere, we just don't know where," I replied.

Shorty nodded. "Yeah, but there is someone who knows."

"Who might that be?" I asked.

"Ignatius Ramos. The Police Chief."

"Fuck me. We're going to have to grab him."

"Take a break," German said. "It looks like we're going to be here for a while yet."

I glanced at Holly and Knocker. Shrugging, I said, "Fine by me."

We left the room and headed back to the cafeteria we'd been using. I'd just got a coffee when Newman appeared. "A word, Kane."

After a moment of hesitation, I nodded. "Sure."

"Not here."

We walked outside and moved to a secluded area. Newman stared hard at me. "What are you up to?"

"What do you mean?"

"You're hiding something," he said to me. "I can feel it."

"Maybe you're just letting things run away with you."

Newman shook his head. "No, I've been in this game too long."

I sighed.

"You asked for my help, remember?" Newman said.

"Fine. Is there anything you've been able to find on Hecate?"

"Nothing," the CIA director said with a shake of his head.

"Have your people dig into the three people on that panel," I said to him.

"Those three? Are you crazy?"

"Why do you think they are on the panel?" I asked him. "Remember I mentioned Anesha Perera?"

"Yes."

"She has friends inside the government who were able to set this up. It's not an inquiry, as such, but a mole hunt. The one stone left unturned."

"Holy shit."

"I need you to help with the intel. However, there is one more thing that you can do. How are your interrogation skills?"

"As good as they ever were."

I nodded. "I'm pleased to hear it. I've got a surprise for you. You need to leave. I'll have Knocker escort you."

"What surprise?"

I shook my head. "That would ruin it."

"I hope it's worth it."

"It will be."

We made our way back inside to the cafeteria, where the others were still waiting.

"Knocker, take Director Newman to the house."

Both he and Holly looked at each other and frowned. "Are you sure, Reaper?"

"Yes, do it."

Knocker got to his feet and said, "Follow me, Director."

Once they were gone, Holly asked, "Are you sure that was a wise idea?"

"He can take over the interrogation."

She looked at her watch. "Let's get back."

———

"I don't know what has happened to Director Newman or Mr. Jensen," German said.

"Newman got a phone call, and Knocker volunteered to drive him to wherever he had to be," Holly lied.

"I see. Oh, well, let's carry on. We're on the home stretch."

Christine Ryan and Holland agreed.

Holland said, "I believe we were up to where you and your assassins were about to kidnap a sworn police commander."

"These assassins, as you call them, helped stop World War Three," I reminded him.

"If you say so."

"Shall I continue?"

"Please do," Christine Ryan said. "If we sit here sniping forever, we'll never get home."

Until we found the missiles or Morozov, Ramos and Garcia were our priority. Ramos was predictable, a creature of habit. Each day, he took the same route home, with the same number of bodyguards, and at the same time.

So, we planned our hit and went to get him.

It was a convoy of three vehicles. The front and rear held armed bodyguards. I had no compunction about taking any of them out, because they were all on the cartel's payroll. The way I saw it, you lie down with dogs, expect to get shot.

The place chosen for the interdiction was a street lined with stores and alleyways, where we could strike and then disappear.

We positioned ourselves on either side of the street—myself, Shorty, and Ted on one side, and Cramer, Hooky, and Manuela on the other. Hooky was in a stolen truck, ready for the convoy. My leg wounds were numb, Ted having hit them with a dose of local.

It was around ten p.m. when the headlights appeared. The convoy was moving fast along the street.

"Hooky, go."

The stolen truck lurched forward from the alley, effectively creating a roadblock. The three SUVs came to a skidding stop and the next part of our plan moved into action.

Me, Cramer, and Ted hurried forward and placed charges on the sides of each SUV. The one on the middle vehicle had less impact than the others. When they detonated, the two bookends were hammered hard and engulfed in flames. The middle SUV, however, had enough charge to knock those inside senseless and dislodge the armored door.

With the damage done, we rushed forward once more. I pulled the damaged door and Ted reached in, hit the target with a hypodermic, and pulled the police commander free of the wreckage.

"I've got the package—fuck."

He had noticed the movement at the same time I did. The guard in the front passenger seat had recovered somewhat and turned with a weapon in his hand.

As fast as a striking rattler, my reflexes had me drawing my handgun, and without hesitation, I fired into the bodyguard's head.

His brains and a whole lot of blood painted the cracked windshield, and he flopped sideways across the console. "Get him out of here," I snapped.

With Ted and Shorty dragging Ramos away from the blazing scene and into the alley, the others and I covered their retreat.

When we ran up to the van, Cramer ripped the door open and said, "Get him the fuck in."

With the silent police commander aboard, we piled in, Cramer driving. Moments later, the vehicle was moving in the opposite direction, away from the carnage we'd caused.

The whole takedown had been quick and rather painless. Now all we needed was the intel.

————

"Wake him up," Cramer ordered.

Ted waved a bottle of smelling salt beneath the man's nose to bring Ramos around. The police commander jerked his head back and opened his eyes, blinking to clear his vision.

"What—what is happening?"

Each of us wore a mask, just as we had when we'd hit the convoy. I stepped in close. The local anesthetic was starting to wear off, and pain was returning to my leg. I slapped his face and said, "You awake, amigo?"

"Who—who are you?"

"Never mind. Let's get this over and done with so we can all go our separate ways."

"Get what done?"

"I want to know where Julio Garcia is," I told him. "He's hidden away in the old part of Havana. Where?"

"I don't know who you are talking about."

"Listen, I don't have the time nor the inclination for a drawn-out interrogation. Tell me what I want to know, or I will turn you loose and have the whole of Cuba know that you cooperated with us."

"You cannot do that."

"Just try me."

"And if I tell you where he is, then Julio will kill me."

I shook my head. "No, we'll kill him."

"How can you be so sure?" Ramos asked.

"Because I'm too busy with Russians to hunt."

"I wish you luck there. They have gone."

My stare grew hard. "What did you say?"

"The Russians have gone. They left yesterday."

Once again, Morozov had slipped through my fucking fingers. That left the missiles. I was loath to ask. "The missiles they had here? Where are they?"

The boom lowered. "They are gone."

"Fuck!"

"Where?" asked Cramer.

"They put the viable ones on a ship and took them to sea," Ramos explained.

"Where to?"

"I do not know."

"What was the name of the ship?" I asked him.

"I don't know."

"Something simple then. Where is Julio Garcia?"

"At the bank," Ramos said.

"The bank? Is that in the middle ,of the earthquake zone?" I asked.

"Yes."

"Draw me a map."

"You are crazy if you think you can get in there and out again," the police commander said.

"You let me worry about that."

For the next hour, Ramos told us all he knew, and we formed our simple plan from that. Go in, hit hard, achieve our goal, and get the hell out.

Once it was sorted, I looked at Manuela. "You aren't coming with us. I need you for something else."

She looked put out, but she'd been in service long enough to know when to follow orders. "What?"

"Sit on Ramos and keep overwatch for us. If it goes wrong, get the hell out. We can't let Ramos go until we're done."

Manuela nodded. "I will do that."

"Thanks. Also, how are your intelligence contacts?"

"Good, actually."

"See if they can help dig up the name of the ship the missiles went on and where Morozov went to."

"I'll take care of it, John. You just come back from there alive."

Intending to go in that night, we spent the next couple of hours preparing. AK-12s, NVGs, frag grenades, body armor, knives, and flashbangs, along with Ted's medical kit and extra ammunition.

With our equipment ready, we geared up and went to war.

CHAPTER 15

I<small>T WAS INDEED LIKE GOING INTO</small> A<small>LEPPO AT THE HEIGHT OF THE</small> war in Syria. We'd all been there, and the rubble and destruction were phenomenal. The old part of Havana was very similar.

Using our van to insert, we pulled up outside the old city perimeter and climbed out. There was limited electricity within the zone, and what was there was brought in for Garcia's complex. The rest of the region was illuminated by fires and old kerosene lamps.

Unfortunately, having no sniper rifle with us, we were constrained to the use of our standard weapons. I rounded the rear of the van just as the Brits were preparing the last of their equipment. With that done, I checked my comms. "Eagle Nest, from Eagle One, copy?"

"Read you, Lima Charlie, One," Manuela replied. "Are you ready to insert?"

"Roger that."

"Around two hundred meters down the street from your location is a two-man checkpoint. You'll need to clear it before you go in."

"Roger that."

Moving forward, utilizing both sides of the street, we drew up to the checkpoint, noting its old-fashioned wood framework wrapped in barbed wire. Off to the side was a fire, burning brightly in a rusted and blackened 44-gallon drum. The two checkpoint guards were standing there talking. "Eagle Nest, this is One."

"Go, One."

"Nest, can you see anyone else in the immediate vicinity? Over."

"Negative, One, you're clear to engage."

"Roger."

"Two, take the one on the right. I'll take the one on the left."

"Copy, One."

Lifting the AK to my shoulder, I sighted on my target and began to count down: "Three...two...one...execute."

WHAP! WHAP!

Oblivious to their impending demise, both guards dropped to the ground, dead.

"Checkpoint clear, we're crossing over."

It sounded like we were going over to the dark side, which, in a way, I suppose we were. Hiding the bodies among piles of debris on the way through, we disappeared into the rubble beyond.

———

"Eagle One, you have an outlier twenty meters ahead of you, sitting behind a mound of trash."

I didn't reply. We were too close. Using hand signals, I motioned Hooky forward. Drawing his combat knife, he handed his other weapon to Shorty. Then he moved forward like a sure-footed cat while we waited for him to do his work.

After Hooky had been lost from our line of vision for a minute or so, we got a static, "X-ray down."

Given the all-clear, we pressed forward, encountering Hooky, who was looking around after stashing the body. Ahead of us sat no end of crumbling apartment complexes.

Crouched beside me, Cramer said, "According to the map, we need to pass through those."

"Roger that. Hooky, you're on point."

"On it, boss."

"Eagle Nest, how are we looking?"

"So far, so good, One. I'll let you know if things change."

"Copy."

Hooky wended his way between mounds of detritus left-over from many years of municipal service failures. We caught up with him just before the first apartment block.

"What's up?" I asked him.

"I thought I saw movement up ahead," Hooky whispered.

"Hold here. Nest, Three thought he detected movement just ahead of our pos. Confirm."

"Wait one." We waited, then, "One, I'm not seeing—hold it. There he is. For some reason, ISR missed it. Thirty meters ahead of your pos, inside a doorway."

"Copy."

I brought up the AK and looked through the sights. At first, there was nothing to see, then after about a minute, he moved.

And I fired.

"Push up."

Inside the first apartment block there had been a massive floor collapse. It was like a hollowed-out concrete tree still standing erect. There was a pathway through the debris to the far wall where a hole had been knocked through into another building. I suddenly felt like I was in World War Two Stalingrad, where the combatants scurried like rats through the ruined city.

It took us ten minutes to negotiate the buildings and break out through the other side onto a winding street. Shorty took point once more, and we traveled steadily deeper into the earthquake zone. Two hours of grueling, slow progress later, we stopped, taking a breather and drinking from our canteens. Ahead of us, on the side of a rise, stood a large archway, like a gate in the night.

Cramer said, "That's it. The opening to the underground is beneath that arch."

I nodded. "Nest, Talk to me."

Manuela was staring at the screen in front of her, taking in all the dots. "Five outriders, One."

From a pouch on the front of my vest, I withdrew a small screen that was linked to the satellite feed. My fingers danced over the touch screen and five dots appeared. "There they are."

"Let's find them," Cramer whispered.

A few minutes later, we had them staked out. Five targets, five shooters. Each operator called in to confirm their ready status.

"Standby," I whispered into my comms. "Three...two... one...execute."

Suppressed weapons spoke and disgorged their payloads. Each target jerked, disappearing as they fell. Breaking from cover, we walked forward to cover new territory. From the satellite overhead, ground-penetrating ISR deciphered the underground tunnels and rooms. I studied my screen for several moments, then slipped it into the pouch on my arm. The target was deep in the middle of the complex of tunnels and cross tunnels.

Locating the entrance didn't take long, but as it wasn't much more than a drain opening, we all had to crouch to gain access. Making our way surreptitiously to avoid detection, we soon drew up before a large doorway at the base of the downward slope. Cramer tried it and found it open. "Here we go."

The tunnels were rock and concrete. That initial entrance door was the only one we encountered. The rest was just a rabbit warren of open corridors.

Utilizing the map provided by our ISR, we moved deeper into the subterranean chambers. The further we ventured, the more cartel soldiers we encountered. Our luck was holding, but once we'd neutralized our sixth assailant, shit hit the fan. The last killer I'd put down had a radio on open channel. Through a burst of static, I heard the frantic calls from another cartel soldier calling in that he'd just found the body of a comrade.

"Had to fucking happen," Cramer said. "Our luck couldn't last forever."

"Yes."

Moments later, the tunnels were crawling with a phalanx of armed killers. Countless fusillades hammered toward us, and we became bogged down, our advance coming to a halt. I pulled the pin on a fragmentation grenade and sent it hurtling further along the tunnel we were in. Unfortunately, its effect wasn't lasting, holding them back for only a few minutes.

Cramer said, "They're pinning us, Reaper."

"It's like they're buying time," I said.

"That's what I was thinking."

"Nest, this is One, copy?"

Through the static, I heard Manuela say, "Just…one. Your transmission is weak."

"We're in heavy contact. They're trying to delay us. Look for another way out."

"Roger, One."

We dispatched several more grenades along the hallway toward the seemingly infinite unseen assailants, and through the reverberations of the blasts, I came to a decision. "We're pulling back, Cramer."

"Roger that."

"Everyone, fall back, leapfrog."

Like the highly experienced team that we were, the second to last man tapped the last man on the shoulder, letting him know when to peel. We reached a junction and held our ground for several minutes. I heard Cramer say, "Shame nobody thought to bring a claymore along for the ride."

"Well, that isn't exactly true," Shorty piped up.

"You fucking ball biter," Cramer said, turning on his man, not sure whether to be angry or grateful. "Set the bastard up."

An expert at his craft, the SAS man soon had the claymore ready to go, a tripwire stretched across the hallway. Before we continued with our withdrawal, Cramer took a smoke grenade and pulled the pin. The hallway began filling with smoke, making it almost impossible to see the wire. "Let's keep moving."

Hustling back toward the entry tunnel, we'd cleared the immediate area when the wire was tripped, and the blast rocked the tunnel complex.

"That'll keep the donkey dicks guessing."

"One, copy?"

"Go ahead, Nest."

"You were right. There is a back door three hundred meters to the rear of the arch. There's movement there as we speak. I count ten, no eleven X-rays."

"Copy, keep an eye on them, Nest. We're moving to that position."

I looked at Cramer. "Good to go?"

"Be fucking happy to get out of this mole's ass."

Making a concerted effort to evade our pursuers, we eventually made it to the entrance door. Pausing, I said into my comms, "Nest, we're at the breach point. Are we going to walk into anything?"

"Negative, One. Breach point is clear. Once you're out, head due east."

When we hit the fresh air, it was still dark, and we started to make our way east using our NVGs. The path through the rubble twisted and turned. There was nothing direct about it. "Nest, update on the target."

"Target is two hundred meters southeast of your current position. You have five X-rays coming your way."

"Copy."

Using mounds of rubble for cover, we took up positions and waited for the cartel killers to arrive. Looming out of the darkness like wraiths from hell, we engaged once they entered the kill zone. Like shooting fish in a barrel, the one-sided confrontation was over in a matter of heartbeats.

For the next ten minutes, we worked our way toward the target who was heading away from us. We were making ground, but not fast enough.

"One, this is Nest."

"Go, Nest."

"At the rate you're traveling, you won't catch the target. Suggest you take an alternative route."

I frowned. "What alternative route, Nest?"

"To your left, One."

I turned my head and saw a jumble of debris and fallen buildings surrounded by a large fence. "Are you sure?"

Hesitation. "Yes. If you want to catch Garcia."

"You don't sound so convincing, Nest."

"There might be a slight drawback with the route, One."

I knew I shouldn't ask. But I did. "What's on the other side of the fence, Nest?"

"It seems our friend Garcia has a novel way of getting rid of his enemies. On the other side of the fence, you'll find jaguars."

"As in the big cat kind of jaguar? You are fucking kidding me," I growled.

"I wish I was. It is the only way you can stop him from getting away. If he does, who knows when you'll get another chance."

"How many?"

"Looks to be five, no six."

"Christ. Wait one, Nest."

I gathered the others and advised them of the situation. "I'm not ordering anyone in there. If we go, it's because we all decide to. Who knows what we'll find."

"It's the only way to get this bastard?" Hooky asked.

"Yes."

"I'm in."

"Shorty?"

"Who's afraid of a bit of pussy? I'm in."

"Can't be scarier than my ex-missus," Ted said. "I'll go."

"Cramer?"

"My team, I go where they do."

I nodded. "All right then."

"Wait," Ted said. "Before we go, how's your leg? I noticed you starting to limp."

"I'll live."

"I didn't ask you that," he prodded me.

"Don't worry. If the Pink Panther starts chasing me, you'll not be able to keep up."

Hooky chuckled. "This is going to be fucking fun. Last one across gets eaten."

"Dickhead," Shorty grunted.

"Nest, copy?"

"Copy, One."

"We're going to take the shortcut."

"Good luck."

We climbed over the rubble and reached the fence. Cramer said to me, "How do you want to do this?"

"Handguns and flashbangs."

"I was thinking along those lines."

"Okay. Everyone, sling your primary weapon. Use handguns only, along with flashbangs. Use the flashbangs as a deterrent first. Your handgun as a last line of defense."

Hooky slung his weapon and grabbed the fence. "Let's get this done."

He climbed over the fence and took a knee on the other side. I was about to start over when Manuela said, "I've got movement inside the fence, thirty meters left and closing your pos."

"Where?" I asked.

"Twenty meters."

"Hooky, contact left. Twenty meters."

"Where?" he growled, bringing up his weapon.

"Wait, it's stopped," Manuela said. "It's backing up."

With a sense of relief, I started over the fence. Once I was down, I crouched next to Hooky until the others joined us. I said, "Everyone remain bunched. No sense inviting them in. With a little luck, they'll think the group is too big."

"You believe that?" Cramer asked me.

"Not one fucking bit."

We started forward, our nerves jangling with the anticipation of what was out there in the dark. "How are we looking, Nest?"

"That one on your left is closing in slowly. The other five are ahead of you in what looks to be a—"

Manuela stopped.

"What?"

"Holy shit. It's a fucking hammer and anvil. These jaguars are clever."

"Are you sure about what you're seeing?"

"If they were human, it's exactly what I'd be saying."

"How far away?" I asked.

"About thirty meters," Manuela replied.

"Keep me updated," I replied. "I said to the others, "Okay, Hooky, get ready with a flashbang. These pussycats are a lot smarter than we first figured. Ted, watch our six."

"Roger that."

We picked a path through debris and plant life. It was almost like a jungle in the city. Then I thought of the victims who had been committed to death inside the perimeter fence and a cold shiver ran down my spine. A bullet was faster.

"One, that Jaguar behind you has closed to around ten meters."

"Copy. Heads up, Ted."

"Oh shit, he's moving," Manuela said, anxiety in her voice. "Straight at you."

"Fuck."

I grabbed a fragmentation grenade and threw it after pulling the pin. "Frag out!"

Everyone dropped to the ground, and a moment later, the grenade detonated. A ball of flame illuminated the compound as it blew into the air. The sound shattered the stillness of the night and echoed off the skeletal buildings.

"Where is it?" Cramer called out.

"It's pulled back. The others have scattered. Lookout, one is coming straight at you from the front."

Hooky pulled the pin on his flashbang and let it go. "Bang out!"

There was another loud crack that hammered out. Through my night vision, I could see Hooky standing with his handgun straight out in front, waiting for the assault. Suddenly, our comms lit up again. "The right! One is coming in from the right!"

No sooner had the words left Manuela's lips than a Jaguar leaped from the shadows and hit Hooky from the side.

"Shit, fuck."

Although he didn't scream, Hooky didn't take the assault quietly. He went down under the weight of the fast-moving feline but rolled with it. He didn't fight it, but drove his handgun into the beast's side and pulled the trigger six times.

Cramer ran to his side and pulled the dead animal off his man. "Are you okay, Hooky?"

"Motherfucker almost had me, boss."

"Get up. We've got to keep moving."

Hooky got to his feet. "Fuck me."

"Nest, I need a sitrep on the other five and the target, over."

"One, the five Jaguars have scattered and backed off. The target and his bodyguards look to have sped up."

"Copy."

"We need to keep moving," I said.

Once more, our tight-knit group moved rapidly. Heads on a swivel, we waited for the next attack to come.

We negotiated an old hotel garden and then a green, scum-filled pool. Pushing on, we came across a jumble of old vehicles and what had once been a playground. It reminded me of the abandoned amusement park in Berlin.

"One, it looks like your friends have overcome their initial wariness and are closing in again. Two behind and three from the front. You are officially surrounded."

"Roger, Nest. Here we go again."

"One, they appear to be behaving differently from last time."

"How so?" I asked.

"It looks like they've adapted and are changing tactics on the run."

"Fucking bullshit," I heard Shorty growl.

"I wish it was," Manuela said. "They're going to hit you all at once."

"Grab your flashbangs, gents. Things are about to get busy. Nest, sitrep on the target."

"Still moving to the exit point, One."

I stood there thinking. We could wait for the Jaguars to hit us, or we could take the fight to them. "All right, on my word, we throw the flashbangs out from our perimeter. Let's fucking confuse them and then make a run for the fence."

"Roger that," said Cramer.

"Pull pins." I waited for a moment and then said, "As soon as they blow, we run. Throw them."

Five flashbangs sailed through the darkness, and moments later, they detonated. "Go! Go! Go!"

We ran through the jungle of debris as best we could, trying not to twist or break ankles on hidden dangers.

"One, keep moving straight. That last blast separated them."

I was trying not to die from falling or feline, so I didn't acknowledge the transmission. Ahead of us, the safety of the fence loomed out of the green haze of my NVGs. So close yet so—

"Incoming from your left. Look out!"

The beast hit me from the side and knocked me from my feet. Losing my grip on the handgun, I knew I was in dire trouble. The snarling animal tried to sink its wicked teeth into my throat. My hands formed fists which delivered a swift uppercut to the creature's chin, then formed an iron grip around its muscular neck when my endeavor failed.

The jaguar's claws ripped at my chest, my body armor protecting my soft flesh from being penetrated.

Figuring that my size had played a role in my survival, I felt blessed that I was a big man. Had I been a regular Joe, the monster would have torn me to shreds.

Now I was stuck. If I let go, the Jaguar would get me. If I didn't and it realized that it could do more harm with its back legs, it could rip my thighs to pieces, maybe hitting an artery, and I would die anyway.

I released my grip long enough to hit it again. However, all it did was further anger the damn thing. I remembered hearing somewhere that the bite force of its jaws was powerful enough to crush a caiman's skull. Probably best to avoid them.

Knowing why the others hadn't come to my rescue, I could hear them fighting their own battles. The screams of Jaguars echoed through the night. If only I could find my handgun. I took a chance and released the grip with my right hand, scrabbling around the ground beneath me, looking for it. I felt my grip slipping on the powerful beast and gave up the search to grab hold of its throat again.

"Can someone give me a fucking hand here?" I cried desperately.

The only answer I received was another Jaguar's scream. I needed to find that gun. I let go with my left hand and repeated the actions I had done with my right, my fingers scrabbling around on the rubble-strewn ground. Then they touched something. At first, I thought it was just another slab of rock, but then I felt it move and my fingers locked onto it. It was the butt of my gun.

Bringing it far enough around, I pressed it against the Jaguar's chest and pulled the trigger five times. I felt the big cat buck with each shot, the bullets driving deep. Such a glorious animal didn't deserve the fight that I was giving it, but in this life-and-death struggle, I was determined that I wasn't going to come out second best.

All the animal's fight left as death claimed it, collapsing on top of me. I rolled the dead weight to the side, my breath coming in great gasps from the sheer exertion. Getting to my feet, I looked around me. My night vision goggles had been dislodged, so I grabbed them and returned them to their correct position in front of my eyes.

I could see the others fighting desperately with another Jaguar. It was on top of a man. I couldn't tell which one, but after a moment, I realized that it was Shorty. I lurched to my feet and stumbled across to them, wanting to help subdue the beast. "Shoot the fucking thing," I growled.

A gunshot echoed through the night and the screams of the Jaguar ceased. We dragged it off Shorty and helped him to his feet. Even through my night vision goggles, I could see that he was bleeding from his arms and a wound on his head.

"Are you okay?" asked Cramer.

"I'll fucking live, boss. Let's get out of you before one of them cunts come back."

"I need to look at your wounds," Ted said.

"It'll have to wait," I said. "Right now, we need to get over that fucking fence."

We covered the last twenty meters to the fence line and started to climb. I could feel the eyes of the remaining jaguars on our backs, but at that point in time, I didn't care where they were. I just knew we needed to get out of our current predicament.

Once on the outside of the perimeter. I said into my comms, "Nest, I need to know where the target is."

"Target is forty meters away from you, coming your direction."

"Roger that." I turned to the others. "Garcia is coming this way. We'll have to check Shorty after. Right now, we need to get Garcia. End this once and for all."

We took up positions on either side of the exit route. Hidden there among rubble, we waited in silence for Garcia and his bodyguards.

Then, out of the green haze, the figures emerged. All were armed and traveling steadily. "Get ready," I said.

We hunkered down, fingers resting on triggers, waiting for them to get within the kill zone. Then I gave the order. "Now."

Our weapons came to life and the cartel men died violent deaths. They jerked wildly under each impact and dropped among the rubble. We came out of cover and put more rounds into them while they were down.

I found Garcia. He was still alive but fading fast. In the darkness, he failed to recognize me. "Who—who are you?" he managed to get out.

"They call me the Reaper," I said coldly. "To you, I'm walking death."

"All down," Cramer said.

"Roger that," I replied.

"Ted, give Shorty a look over before we pull out."

"Copy, boss."

"Nest, copy?"

"Copy, One."

"Shut down and we'll meet you at the RV point."

"Will do. By the way, I have news about our Russian friends. Will fill you in when you get to the RV."

"Copy. One out."

I turned to the others. We still had work to do.

CHAPTER 16

OUR SMALL TEAM WAS CONSTANTLY ON THE MOVE, SLEEPING wherever we could find a bed—currently an apartment complex the Americans used as a safehouse. We'd arrived at a quiet time of year, the unit thankfully vacant. We didn't have to mind our manners while we were there.

Arriving in the underground garage, we found ourselves moving slowly, each of us feeling our own level of physical and mental exhaustion. Some of us carrying injuries. We were pretty hammered. Approaching our vehicle, Manuela was carrying a small go-bag and joined us as we began carrying our kit to the apartment. Crossing to Shorty, she began helping Ted to patch him up as best they could. Cramer and I sat in a corner, a couple water bottles on the table in front of us, forming a pool of condensation around their bases. We were comparing notes.

Not long after, Ted came over to us. "We need to get Shorty out of here to the carrier where they can take better care of him. Some of those cuts need stitching and proper care. Who knows what shit is in them? I've given him some antibiotics, but it's best to be safe, boss."

Cramer nodded. "Leave it to me."

"Don't listen to him, boss, I'm fucking fine. Take more

than fucking Garfield to put me out of fucking action. Damn fucking cat, fucked up thing it fucking is."

Cramer gave Ted a querying look. The operator shrugged. "Pain meds. He's as high as a kite."

"Leave it with me, Ted, I'll get him out."

Cramer looked at me. "I'll have to radio the carrier."

The carrier to which he was referring was the HMS Queen Elizabeth. She was in the Caribbean on a *tour*. When in fact, since the discovery of missiles had leaked, she had been stationed there just in case.

Manuela joined us. "I told you I had news."

I nodded. "Shoot."

"GROM believes that Morozov has gone to Belarus to oversee the Russian deployment."

"That's going to be tricky," I said. "They're obviously moving things up."

"From what you've told me," Cramer said. "The missiles are on the move. Russian troops on the frontier, Morozov in Belarus, Lash moving a few chess pieces around. They're getting ready for war."

"They just need one more piece to fall into place," I said.

"Which is?"

"Pridham," I said.

"For that piece, he needs to win the election," Cramer said.

"Ah—" Manuela said.

"What is it?" I asked her.

"Since the bombs went off in London, he's shot up in the polls. It looks like he could romp it in."

"Shit, I hope Knocker is on top of it. Is there any good news?"

"We know where the scientist is. If you are able to question him, then you might find out where the missiles are."

"Then let's pick the twat up," Cramer said.

"That is where the problem lies. He's in the Russian embassy."

"Then we'd better get the bastard out," I said. "Fucking pronto."

"Please don't tell me you affected a kidnapping from sovereign soil," German said.

"Okay, I won't," I replied.

"Thank God for that. How did you get him?"

"We dressed up as Russians and walked into the embassy and kidnapped him."

"Oh, Christ," Holland said.

I said, "There was no other way to do it. We needed to know the location of the missiles so we could stop them."

"Who knew about this illegal incursion?"

"The six of us here and the SAS boys. And the Russians."

"Of course they do. There would be no hiding it after the fact."

I gave him a pained expression. "Not exactly."

"Shit."

———

Cuba's Russian embassy was in Havana, the central part was a tall tower block that somewhat resembled one of the Transformers standing guard over a hidden secret.

What we were about to do was illegal in so many ways, and if caught, I could guarantee that we would disappear into a dark hole somewhere in Siberia after being paraded on Russian television.

The intention was for Cramer and I to turn up at the front door. We were dressed in suits and had fake papers identifying us as FSB. Our main problem with that was going to be that since Russia's return to the KGB, identity papers reflecting the change had been reissued to almost all of their officers.

Ted and Hooky were going in through the tunnels beneath the embassy. There's always tunnels. I mean, you've seen the movies, right? Their job was to secure them for exfil because we had no intention of going out the same way we'd come in.

To gain access, however, we had to get through the checkpoint at the main gates. The guards on duty stopped us before we could enter, demanding, then scrutinizing our papers. One of them, a middle-aged man, looked at the papers and then at me. His head tilted to the side and then he said, "These are the wrong papers."

"I know," I said. "We've only just arrived here. When we left Moscow, they were still busy transferring them over into the new ones and had run out, and we missed out. Hence, we're still stuck with our old ones."

He still looked skeptical but accepted our excuse and let us through. Our confident strides along the driveway told anyone watching that we were authorized to be there. Climbing the short flight of steps, we entered the main building. There was an X-ray machine and a metal detector ahead of us. Without hesitation, we took our weapons and placed them in a tray so they could be sent along beside us. When we walked through each scanner, nothing untoward happened.

Once we were through, we collected our weapons and continued walking toward the elevator bank. "Nest, we are in. Need you to shut down the security cameras and find Kahn."

"Copy. Will shut them down in three...two...one... cameras down. Kahn is on the third floor in an office toward the rear of the building."

"Copy. Moving to that location."

Entering the first elevator to arrive, Cramer hit the button. We had a low conversation in Russian which helped our cover, but it wasn't fluent. However, being passable in situations like this was sometimes enough.

The smooth passage of the elevator took us closer to the floor we needed, then slowed before jerking the final distance to a stop. When the doors slid open, we stepped out into an open-plan office area with a walkway along a single wall.

Eyes darted in our direction before returning to their

work. My guess was that this was an intelligence hub. Intelligence was gathered from different regions—locations such as North America, the Caribbean, and various other countries—before being analyzed, encoded, and sent on to Russia.

I hesitated as I looked around. Cramer stood just off my shoulder. A man in a suit looked over at us, and for a moment, I thought he wasn't going to do anything. But he changed his mind. "You. What are you doing?"

"What has it got to do with you?" I asked.

He gave me an indignant look. "I am in charge here."

"Congratulations."

His expression dirtied somewhat. "What are you doing here?"

"There is a scientist here. We are here for him."

"Where are your papers?"

"We don't need to show you our papers," Cramer said.

"I said show me your papers. That is an order."

"Do you know who we are?" I asked.

"I have no idea," the man replied. "Nor do I care."

"We are KGB. You will not disobey our orders. You will tell us where the scientist is, or we will report you to the president himself." My voice was harsh and firm.

I saw the man hesitate, his facade starting to crack. "I need to see orders."

Shaking my head, I said, "I guess a good holiday in Siberia will suffice after this hot climate."

"I will take you to him."

"Just tell us. I'm sure we can find him ourselves."

He pointed to a door at the far end of the room. "Through there is a hallway. He is in the room at the end."

"What is your name?" I asked him.

"My name is Rostov," he replied.

"Thank you. I will be sure to mention your cooperation."

Cramer and I turned away from the man and left him standing there with his nervous thoughts. We strode purposefully to the door and passed through.

Once it closed behind us, Cramer said, "That was fucking hairy."

"I agree. I thought we were done there for a moment. Now let's find this guy and get the fuck out of here."

As we traveled the length of the hallway, we passed three doors on either side before reaching the one we wanted. I knocked briefly before turning the knob. The door snicked open, and we entered.

Kahn was standing, staring out the window. He turned to face us. "Who are you?"

"We're here to take you out of Cuba," I replied.

He frowned. "What do you mean take me out of Cuba?"

"We received orders from General Shatov. He wants us to accompany you back to the motherland before everything starts to happen."

"But I was talking to General Morozov this morning and he mentioned nothing of this."

I nodded. "It's last minute. But we must hurry because there is a plane waiting."

"Show me your orders."

"We don't have time," Cramer said.

"Then you'd better make time," Kahn said defiantly.

We were getting nowhere fast. In my ear, I heard Manuela say over comms, "Eagle One, I just intercepted a phone call going out. It was made to Morozov in Belarus. In short, your cover has been blown. I'd get out of there now."

"You get that?" I asked Cramer in English. There was no point in maintaining the façade.

He nodded and took out his handgun. "I got it."

Realization came to Kahn's face. "You're not Russian."

"And you're a fucking terrorist," I growled. "Secure him and let's get the fuck out of here. Nest, I need a way out."

"Back wall of the room you're in has a hidden door behind the bookcase."

"Really?"

"Hand on heart."

I hurried over to the bookcase while Cramer watched the

door and the hallway beyond. I attempted to move it, but it remained in place. "I don't suppose you know where the release catch is?"

"Sorry, you're on your own."

I turned to look at Kahn. "What about you?"

"Reaper, they're coming," Cramer said.

"Stall them."

"If you say so," he replied and opened fire.

Meanwhile, I strode purposefully over to Kahn, gun in hand. "I'm not leaving you behind alive. Make your choice."

He hesitated. Then finally drew his own conclusion that I wasn't fooling around. "Third shelf, second book on the right."

I rushed back and pulled the appropriate book, hearing the audible click through the gunfire. I pulled the bookcase, and it swung back, revealing the staircase.

"Let's go," I called over to Cramer.

When Cramer slammed the door, an immediate fusillade of bullets hammered into it, busting through the veneer. Cramer grabbed Kahn and growled, "Hurry the fuck up, mate. No time to waste here."

I led the way down the stairs while Cramer closed the door behind us. Moments later, it opened again, and we could hear voices calling out in Russian.

"Help me!" Kahn cried out. "We are down—"

Cramer gave him a solid crack across the back of the head with his handgun, but not hard enough to knock him silly. "Shut the fuck—"

Gunfire erupted from above and bullets ricocheted around the stairwell. "Keep moving," I snarled.

We continued our frantic pace down, taking the concrete stairs two at a time. Now was not the time to slip and break an ankle.

I said into my comms, "Ted, Hooky, copy?"

"Roger, One."

"We're on our way down hot. Get ready."

"We can hear."

With Cramer pushing our prisoner in front of him, making sure he kept up with my rapid rate of descent, we eventually reached the basement where the tunnels were located. Relief washed over me when I saw our backup ahead.

As we drew level with them, Ted said to me, "Keep going, we'll cover you."

They were armed in full kit and carried suppressed AK-12s. Even as we moved farther along the tunnels, I heard them start firing. In my ear, Manuela said, "We've got Cuban police vehicles coming toward the embassy. Be aware they might try to set up roadblocks."

Behind us, the gunfire intensified. I heard Cramer say, "Ted, sitrep."

"We're on our way to you, boss. These pricks are getting serious. We'll be coming in hot."

The tunnel came out in a large underground parking garage. The van was parked there, ready to go. So were three Russian security guards. "Shit."

My weapon came up and I opened fire without hesitation. The first guard went down with two rounds in his chest. The others brought their weapons up and opened fire, forcing me to take cover behind a parked vehicle. Bullets hammered into its panels and one of the windows blew out, spraying glass throughout the vehicle.

Cramer joined me, pushing Kahn ahead of him. Kahn slammed into the side of the vehicle and slid down onto the concrete, sitting with his back pressed against it.

Firing at the shooters until our weapons were empty and the slides locked back, Cramer and I both reloaded and were about to start again when the others appeared. They walked forward, AKs raised and firing steadily at the two guards.

The first of the two security men appeared and then disappeared when a bullet punched into his brain. The second man, knowing the position he was in, dropped his weapon and raised his hands in surrender. "Don't shoot, Comrade."

I walked forward and barked, "Turn around."

He turned and I hit him. He dropped like a stone and lay still. Looking back at the others, I said, "Get Kahn in the van."

Moments later, we were all in the van and just in time, too. The pursuers emerged from the tunnels, finally closing the distance between us, and opened fire.

Bullets hammered into the rear of the van as we retreated toward the surface. The van launched into the air as it cleared the crest of the driveway, with Hooky behind the wheel. Then I made my Arnold Schwarzenegger call. "Nest, get to the chopper!"

"You didn't just do that," she replied.

"Do what?"

"You know."

Then I realized. "Do it."

"Roger that. See you there."

The next call I made was to the helicopter. "Snake Eyes, Snake Eyes, this is Eagle One, copy?"

"Copy, Eagle One."

"We're about ten mikes out from the RV and possibly coming in hot, over."

"Roger that. We'll be ready."

"You will not get away with this?" Kahn said savagely.

"Let's see, huh," Cramer said to him. "Where are the missiles?"

"I have no idea."

"Now, later, it doesn't really matter. You'll talk."

"I will never betray my country," he snarled.

I was about to join the conversation when the world turned turtle. As if out of nowhere, an armored SUV smashed into the side of the van and flipped it.

CHAPTER 17

THE SMASH RANG EVERY BELL IN THE VAN. MY HEAD SPUN AS I fought to remain conscious and drag myself back from the depths of darkness. "Kane, you alright?"

"Yeah, I think so," I replied, trying to place the voice before I realized that it was Cramer.

"The fuckers hit us from the side. I need you in the game," the SAS man demanded, taking over command.

"Give me something to shoot with."

He shoved an AK in my hands and said, "There. It's got a full mag. Now, follow me."

Before I even moved, I could hear gunfire. "Who's that?"

"Ted."

Apparently, I'd lost consciousness after all. I followed Cramer out through the back and sat leaning against the van. "Where's Hooky?"

"I'm here, buddy. Glad to see you're awake."

The gunfire intensified. "Who are they?"

"Russians," Cramer replied. "They look to be mercenaries."

"Igoshin's people."

"Looks like."

My head started to clear, and I peered around the van. The Russians, using their wrecked SUV for cover, were close.

No wonder the volume of the shooting was so high. I wasn't imagining it.

I brought the AK up, aiming and squeezing the trigger toward the SUV. The AK hammered into my shoulder as rounds spewed from its muzzle. I had to rein myself in before I blew through the whole magazine. Beside me, Ted fired at an unseen target. A cry of pain was heard, and another Russian was out of the fight.

"Hooky," Cramer called. "Get us some more ammo."

"On it, boss."

He disappeared inside the van, reappearing with a canvas bag with full magazines. "Yo, ammo up."

Just in time because I had run dry. "I'm out."

Hooky threw me a couple of magazines. I reloaded and started shooting again. Cramer said, "We need to get the fuck out of here."

"Here," Hooky said and threw his boss a fragmentation grenade along with a smoke grenade.

Cramer pulled the pin and threw the frag first. The grenade bounced into the SUV and came to rest near the front tire. "Frag out!"

It blew with a deafening roar. We were all hunkered down went it went up, but we still felt the warmth of the blast as it washed over us.

Next up, Cramer threw the smoke grenade and waited for it to start producing. "All right, let's go."

Coming to our feet, we started to flee from the wreck site. Cramer led the way while Ted brought up the rear with Kahn. Hooky was in front of me as we reached the safety of an alley mouth. "Keep moving," Cramer said.

I said, "I need to reach out to the helicopter."

"Do it."

"Snake Eyes, this is Eagle One, copy?"

"Roger, One, read you Lima Charlie."

"We're in need of immediate extraction, over."

"Say again, One."

"We need extraction. Cannot make the RV."

"Roger that," came the reply. "I'll need coordinates for a new LZ."

"Wait one." I looked around. "Cramer, we need a new LZ."

We scanned the vicinity surrounding our location. Stretching out his arm and pointing his finger, Cramer said, "There."

I saw where he was indicating. The rooftop of an apartment block to our east. "Get the coordinates to the helicopter. They need to pick Manuela up first."

Changing the direction we were traveling, staying in cover where we could, we headed toward the apartment block. Off to the west, we could hear the beat of the helicopter blades as it moved into position to collect Manuela.

My leg began to ache, but the discomfort was manageable, unlike the previous days. It seemed like a positive sign it was healing. The edges of the wounds were beginning to itch, and I had to restrain myself from scratching and causing further damage.

Moving quickly, we soon arrived at the base of the apartments.

"Inside," Cramer said.

We jogged across to the main entrance and went inside. There were only four flights of stairs to climb, but it felt like more and was hard going after the distance we'd just covered and the constant operating we'd all endured.

Bursting out onto the rooftop into bright sunlight, I immediately got onto the comms and said, "Snake Eyes, this is Eagle One. We are at the RV, I say again, we are at the RV."

"Roger, One. We're five mikes out. Hang in there."

"Hey, boss," Ted called out. "Over here."

Cramer and I ran across the rooftop and peered over the edge. Below us, on the ground, a group of armed men was running toward the building. I counted at least ten. They stopped short of the apartment block, their leader waving an arm around like he was directing traffic. Then they split up.

"They're coming up," Cramer said. "Hooky, take up position at the landing. Ted, scout the perimeter and see if there is another way up."

"Got it, boss."

Now we had to wait.

I went back to the edge and looked down again. The distant squeal of tires drew my attention, and I saw vehicles approaching at speed. As they grew closer, I could see that they were police. Pulling up, they remained with their vehicles, securing the perimeter.

Ted came back to us. "The way we came is the only way onto the rooftop."

"Hooky," Cramer called. "You're the gatekeeper."

"Roger that."

"Eagle One, Snake Eyes is two minutes out."

"Roger, Snake Eyes. LZ is hot."

"Contact!" Hooky called out and opened fire.

I ran across to the doorway. Cramer remained with Kahn, and Ted watched the perimeter from the rooftop. In the distance, I could hear the approach of the helicopter.

Positioning myself opposite Hooky, I waited for him to stop firing. Bullets ripped through the space between us. "Do you have a frag?" I asked him.

Hooky shook his head. "Flashbang only."

"That'll do. Give them something to think about."

He took the flashbang and pulled the pin before throwing it through the opening. I could hear it bouncing on the steps and the yelp of alarm before it detonated.

Leaning around the corner of the doorway, I sprayed an almost full magazine down the stairs. Once the mag was empty, I dropped the AK and pulled my handgun. Hooky took advantage of the lull and sent his own rounds down the opening.

Behind us, the helicopter came in. It was a Merlin HC3 and touched down on the rooftop. Sprinting for the safety of the helo, we climbed aboard, Kahn having no other option but to get on as well.

Moments later, the pilot had the helicopter lifting and turning away from the rooftop and on the way to the carrier.

I looked across the bay and saw Manuela. She gave me a nod and a smile. I was glad to be leaving Cuba, but there was still a lot of work to be done. *"I have a question," Christine Ryan asked. "The last we heard, you still had Ramos. What happened to him?"*

"Manuela cut him loose when she left for the RV."

"How do you mean, cut him loose?"

"She set him free. Nothing sinister. There was no need to do otherwise."

"I see, continue."

Shorty was already aboard the carrier, and each of us checked in on him once we had cleaned ourselves up. He was hooked up to an IV line pumping antibiotics into his system. The fever he had broke and was on the way down. The other new addition to his skin was about fifty stitches and staples in various wounds. He looked at Cramer and said, "I'll be back in the fold in a few days, boss. Don't leave without me."

"You just get better, Shorty. Let me worry about the rest."

"Do you need anything?" I asked Shorty.

"Nope, I'm good. Drugs, painkillers, and even a hot doctor."

"I hope you're not talking about me," a young woman with dark hair said as she came up behind us.

"Not me, Doc," Shorty replied.

"Is he doing all right, Doc?" Cramer asked.

"He'll be fine in a few weeks."

"I don't have that much time," Shorty said, a concerned expression on his face. "I need to get back with my team, Doc."

"You are going nowhere except home to recover."

"Boss?"

"Doctor's orders, Corporal."

"Fuck. Sorry, Doc."

She took his temperature and said, "It's still coming down. But you need rest. Now, gentlemen, if you please?"

"Thanks, Doc," Cramer said, and we trooped out after saying goodbye to Shorty.

Making our way to the mess, we all prepared to indulge in a large feed, the first one for a few days. Manuela met us there, having spent a few hours catching up on some sleep. After a shower and fresh clothes, she looked a far cry from the operator we'd been working with over the past few days.

Our plates piled high with eggs and lasagna, we ate until we were satiated and then followed with strong coffee. When we were about finished, the ship's intelligence officer came and found us. His name was Lieutenant Commander Royston. "Your man is ready to go," he said to us. "If you'll follow me."

Manuela, Cramer, and I followed him down a level and across to the port side. "He's in there," Royston said as he stopped outside of a hatch.

I nodded. "Come on in, sir, you might learn something."

"From all I've heard you blokes have been up to, I'm not sure I want to learn," he replied gravely. He scratched at his neatly trimmed beard. "But I'm a naturally curious person."

We entered the room and found Kahn seated at a stainless-steel table. He'd washed and been provided with a clean pair of gray coveralls. He was also wearing handcuffs. He looked up and said, "I demand to speak to your commanding officer. I have been kidnapped from the Russian embassy in Cuba."

"I'm sorry, sir," Royston replied. "The Commodore is a very busy man."

I stood in front of the table. "Okay, Sepp, where are the missiles?"

"I don't know what you are talking about."

"They were moved because the new motors were defective and didn't have the range," I reminded him.

He frowned and then suddenly realized that he'd seen me before. "You are him. You were there with the general."

"I was. I heard you telling him. Then you said something about Matanzas. But they aren't there. They were put on a ship. What—"

In that moment realization dawned on me the answer to the question. "Matanzas. That is the name of the ship, isn't it?"

Kahn shook his head, but his eyes gave it away.

"Where is it headed?" I asked.

"No, you have it wrong," he said desperately.

"No, I don't, where is the fucking ship?"

"I don't know," Kahn replied.

I looked at Royston. "Are you able to help?"

He nodded. "If it's out there, we'll find it."

Following Royston from the room, we stopped outside the door. I said to Royston. "What can you tell me about the Russians and their posture?"

"They're still riding the Polish border, and they've built up forces on the Finnish one as well."

"Tell me about Finland."

"I can do better than that. Follow me."

Once more, we accompanied Royston. This time, he led us to a cabin equipped with screens, computers, and intelligence officers. After a brief wait, he projected a map onto a large screen. With a few clicks of a remote, the focus shifted to Eastern Europe.

Royston said, "This is the Russian border with Poland. They have moved four divisions along the border. Around forty-eight thousand troops."

"The news was reporting around three hundred."

"Propaganda," Royston said. "

"So what do they have?"

"Mechanized and ground troops. What is interesting is what they've done on the Finland border. They have put four divisions along there. Two mechanized and two ground troops. However, we're getting reports of another three divisions spread out fifty kilometers behind the lines."

"They're going to move on Finland," I said.

"That would be my guess."

"What is the government thinking?" I asked.

"They're convinced that the target is Poland. Apparently, they have intelligence which corroborates it."

"Fucking head shed," Cramer growled.

"I agree."

I stared at the map and then at the Russian troop placements. "Where is the Northern fleet?"

"Most of their surface fleet is in the Barents Sea. Except with some of her Oscar IIs, a Yassen, and some Akulas."

"They could keep anyone out of the Baltic if they wanted to," I pointed out. "They could slip in there, sit on the bottom, and wait. What about Russian ships in St. Petersburg?"

"A couple of destroyers and a few landing ships."

"I see it," Cramer said.

I nodded. "Me too. They're going to move on Helsinki by land and sea. Like a pincer movement. Get the forces into the city and hold it until the other divisions can get there."

Royston said, "No one in the government will move until after the election."

"Or not at all if Pridham gets in," I said.

"Since the devastation caused by the bombings in London, he's been screaming for all British military to be brought home for border protection. The civvies are starting to think he might have something."

"Polls?"

"Show him with a substantial lead."

"What does his party think?" I asked.

"They don't like it, but they dislike the current government more. I believe that they are hoping once he is elected, they'll be able to control him."

"Let's hope it doesn't get that far."

———

I called Holly. "How are things on your end?"

"Things are progressing," she replied but failed to provide any further details.

"You know they're going after Finland, don't you?"

"According to our intelligence, Poland is the most likely target."

"I don't give a fuck about intel, Holly. What does your gut tell you?"

"My gut tells me they are wrong. But tell me about you."

I gave her a quick rundown. "We've got to find the missiles first, and then I'm going to Belarus after Morozov."

"By the way, we've located our missing general. Or rather, we know where he is."

"Where?"

"He's in the UK."

"Name?" I asked.

"Oleg Zhirkov."

"At last, we know them all," I said, not feeling the relief I thought I would feel once we had that name.

"Yes, but there are still a few pieces of the jigsaw to come together."

"Any idea on who Pridham is? What his link is to it all?"

"Denis Sobolev," Holly replied. "Pridham's grandfather was hardline KGB and commanded their infiltration wing for a while. He was responsible for placing covert operators into the US and all across Europe. It looks like he shipped his family off to the UK soon after Pridham was born. Gave them new names and IDs and had them set just for this moment."

"Talk about playing the long game."

"Exactly. Now, what can I do for you?"

"First off, thanks for Manuela."

"My pleasure. I assume she worked out?"

I smiled to myself. "You could say that."

"I see."

"Is Slick there?"

"I'll just get him."

"And, Holly?"

"Yes?"

"Thanks for everything."

"Can't have my second-best man getting killed, can I?" I could hear the humor in her voice.

"Second-best?"

"Sorry, but when it comes to operating, Raymond does like to get down in the mud with the bad guys."

I grinned. "I can't argue with that."

"*You really said that?*" Knocker asked as he reentered the room. *Holly looked at him. "What are you doing back here?"*

"*All good. I did what I had to do," he replied. "You said that? About me? That's about the nicest thing you've said."*

I rolled my eyes.

"*Well, credit where credit is due, Raymond."*

Knocker looked at me. "Then she had to do that."

I nodded.

Holly frowned. "What?"

"*You called him Raymond," I replied.*

"*What's wrong with that?"*

"*Hates it. Only his mother and—"*

"*Ex-wives call me Raymond," Knocker finished.*

"*I never knew."*

"*Well, now you do. Just had to go and ruin a beautiful moment."*

"*Are you all quite done?" German asked impatiently.*

"*Depends," said Knocker.*

German frowned. "On what?"

"*On whether there are more good things to be said about me."*

"*Sit down and shut up, Ray," I growled.*

"*Not you too, Reaper. And here I thought we were friends."*

He sat down and crossed his arms.

"*Now, let's continue," German said.*

"*Reaper, you rang?"*

"I need your help, Slick, if you can manage it."

"You know me, Reaper. I'm an octopus when it comes to a keyboard."

"Good man. We need to find a ship called the Matanzas.

And Morozov is in Belarus. Find him, keep an eye on him until I can get there."

"Consider it done."

"Thanks, Slick."

———

Twelve hours later, he was back with good news. "I've found the ship you're after. It's off the East Coast of the US. I'm guessing that it is positioning itself for a strike on Washington. It is sailing under a new name. The Utah. It took a bit, but I found it eventually."

"I need to get on that ship," I said.

"Why? Just have the US Navy sink her."

"Because we need to know if the missiles are there. No sense in just assuming and then find out after the fact they're not."

"I guess it makes sense."

"What about Morozov?" I asked.

"He was far easier of the two to find. But he's not in Belarus," Slick said. "He's in Helsinki."

"Shit, do you know where?"

"No, they're up to their old tricks with the cameras again. But he's there all right. I'll send you what I have."

"Fine, keep digging. Thanks, Slick, we couldn't do this without you."

Disconnecting the call, I went in search of the others, finding them drinking coffee in the onboard cafeteria. Shorty had already been evacuated and was on his way back to the UK for specialist treatment.

"We have the ship. Slick said it's been renamed the *Utah*. He's also going to send us everything that he found on Morozov's location. Now all we need to do is make a plan and get aboard that ship."

Cramer said. "Ship interdiction, I'm thinking two teams, Reaper."

"One to secure the bridge and one to secure the ship," I agreed.

"Would you like some advice from someone who has never done a ship interdiction before?" Manuela asked.

Cramer nodded. "Shoot, there is no right or wrong when planning. Just ideas."

"Three teams. One for the bridge and two for the ship and missiles. I'm guessing that Grigori Igoshin has people on that ship. If not, no harm. If he does, you'll be grateful for the extra firepower."

I looked over at Cramer. "She could be right."

Ted said, "The more the merrier, boss."

The SAS commander looked at Hooky. "Well?"

"I saw Smitty earlier. They usually run heavy."

Cramer focused his gaze back on me. "Looks like three teams it is. I'll go and find Smitty."

"And I'll find Royston. He'll be able to help."

"What do you want me to do?" Manuela asked.

"Once the intel comes through from Slick, go over it and see if anything jumps out at you."

"Roger that."

"Let's do it."

CHAPTER 18

WE CAME ONTO THE SHIP IN THREE DIFFERENT PLACES. I CAME on with Cramer's team over the stern. This was his show. I was there for the ride. Ken *Smitty* Smith had a heavy team which he broke into two groups of six. One team came over the side amidships while the other came over closer to the bow.

Kneeling as I hit the deck, I awaited orders. Soon, everyone checked in, and the operation gained momentum. Each team had distinct mission parameters. The two deck-teams led the way, silently neutralizing multiple guards. Team two remained on deck while team three descended below. In the meantime, we took the bridge.

Failing to find any external stairs, we had to gain access to the superstructure to locate the internal stairwell. Beginning our journey, I was second in line behind Hooky. He led us upward, our rubber-soled boots silent on the metal treads. On each landing, he stopped, checked above, and then continued. The stairwell opened out onto the bridge, where we found four men on duty, plus a guard.

The element of surprise caught everyone off guard, yet the guard chose to take his chances. Our UCIWs, compact versions of the M4 Assault Rifle, were at the ready. Suppressors ensured that when Ted fired at the guard, the sound remained confined to the bridge. The man's cry of pain echoed briefly before he collapsed. Ted swiftly approached to confirm that the threat had been neutralized.

"Who are you?" asked the officer of the watch.

"Just shut the fuck up and do as we say," Cramer said.

I said, "Just keep the ship moving as though nothing is wrong. We'll be gone soon."

Behind me, I could hear Cramer checking in with the other two teams. Everything seemed to be going according to plan. I stared at the first officer and asked, "Is Grigori Igoshin on this ship?"

The white-uniformed man shook his head. "No. No, no one by that name is here."

"Are his men on this ship?"

The first officer nodded. "Yes."

"How many?"

"There are fifteen."

"Where are the ones who aren't on duty?" I asked.

"In their quarters," he replied.

I pointed at the ship's layout diagram on the wall. "Show me."

The first officer hurried across to the wall. With a trembling finger, he touched the second deck layout, indicating several cabins at the end of a long corridor, and said, "There."

"Cramer."

"I'll let them know."

For the next 10 minutes, the other two SAS teams secured the whole ship. Apart from the sentries that had been on duty and the guard on the bridge, there were no other enemy casualties. Once the ship was secured and all the nonessential crew and guards were locked in a hold, we went about securing the missiles with explosives.

Smitty called in half an hour later and said, "All the missiles are secure. We've just finished planting the explosives on them."

"What about the scuttling charges?" I asked.

"Scuttling charges are set, Eagle Two."

"Roger that. Get everyone topside now." I turned to the first officer. "If I were you, I'd get everyone off this ship. There are numerous explosives set to blow, and it will go up. There will be no stopping them, so don't even try. The best course of action is for you and all your crew to abandon ship. I don't care what you do about Igoshin's men."

"But you can't do this," the first officer stammered. "It is against all maritime laws."

"So is transporting nuclear missiles with the intent to launch them," I pointed out.

Receiving word that everybody was back on deck, I turned once again to the first officer and said, "Make your decision. We're leaving now."

Cramer issued his orders, and we began to vacate the bridge, retracing our steps down to the deck. Gathering at the side, we awaited our pick-up. The SAS commander said, "All right, everyone over the side. Let's get out of here."

Going over the rail, we rappelled down into two waiting boats, which pulled away as soon as everyone was safely aboard.

Cramer looked at the face of his luminescent watch. He turned to the man at the helm of our boat and said, "Stop here."

The man pulled back on the throttles, powering the boat down to leave us rocking and bobbing on the vessel's wake. I looked through the dark at Cramer. He said, "Any minute now."

From our position off the ship's stern, we could see movement on deck. Several lifeboats were deployed, dropping over the side. The hapless crew was making their break. Then, as they were pulling away from the ship, the *Matanzas* exploded, going up in a roar of orange flame. Our mission was successful. We hadn't sustained any casualties, and the missiles were now on their way to the bottom of the ocean, destroyed on-site.

Cramer said, "Job well done, Reaper."

"That it is. Now, all I have to do is get Morozov."

The general, however, had one final surprise up his sleeve. The ship must have been under surveillance because, seemingly out of nowhere, a helicopter appeared.

"Fuck me," Cramer growled. "These pricks think of everything. Get this fucking boat moving now."

Tracers lit up the sky as the helicopter opened fire. Red streak-like lasers ripped into the sea around us. I heard the boat driver cry out as one of them punched into him from behind. He slumped forward and then fell to the deck. I heard Cramer shout, "Hookey, take the helm."

Coming forward, Hookey grabbed the helm before the boat could go wildly out of control. The boat's second crewman jumped on a minigun and began firing at the helicopter. Green tracers crossed with red, making pretty patterns across the starry sky. Hooky started to wave the boat from side to side, making it more difficult for the helicopter to hit us. But this created a problem for the crewman on the minigun.

Another pass from the helicopter chewed gouges of fiberglass from the side of the boat. Ricochets whizzed all around us and it was a miracle that none of us were hit. All we could do was hang on and hope for the best.

In the night sky, the helicopter turned on a dime and came sweeping back. Once more, the red tracers from its mini gun ripped through the night. This time, it overshot, sending the rounds harmlessly into the sea.

Cramer slapped the crewmen on the back and said, "If you're going to shoot that fucking thing down, do it now. Because our luck isn't going to hold all bloody night."

"Then tell your man to hold the boat fucking still," the crewman shot back.

"Hookey. Give him a chance."

"Who? John Wayne or the fucking helicopter, boss?"

"Just keep it on a straight line." Cramer turned back to the gunner and said through the wind, "Here's your chance, don't fuck it up."

The helicopter swept back in, and the minigun opened fire once more. Hooky gripped the boat's wheel, maintaining a steady course as the minigunner aimed for the target.

But the red tracers from the helicopter bore down on us like fiery arrows on a collision course. The minigun's roar echoed, a relentless train hurtling toward us. I glanced over the side, briefly considering a leap to safety. After all, nothing says adventure like dodging bullets on the high sea.

Then, in an orange ball of flame, the helicopter exploded, and you could almost hear the collective sigh of satisfaction over the roar of the boat motors.

"Good man," Cramer said, the relief evident in his voice. "Bloody good man."

"Slick, have you found him yet?" I asked, hoping that he had good news.

"I can tell you two things, Reaper," he said to me. "The first is that Morozov is now in Minsk. The second is I have no idea where he is."

"Now that the missiles are gone, I need to go to Minsk. Lash isn't going to let this stop his plans. The only thing likely to work will be to take out his remaining command structure."

"You don't really want to go to Minsk, do you, Reaper?" His voice was unsure.

"If that's where Morozov is, then, yes, I do. Besides, these people are the only ones who know the full plan."

"You'll need a good cover."

"Agreed," I replied. "Send me press paperwork. I'll go in as a freelance journo."

"John?"

"Hey, Holly. What's up?"

"I was listening in. I don't like the idea, but if you must go, take Manuela with you. She will thrive in that environment."

"It's too much risk," I replied.

"Give her the chance to make that decision herself, John."

"Okay, I'll do that."

"What are you going to do when you find Morozov?"

"Gather intel and then kill him."

"Just make sure you're not on the other end of the equation, John. If something happens inside Belarus, I can't help you."

"Yes, ma'am."

"Good luck."

I turned my attention back to Slick. "Can you do that for me?"

"Yes, I'll find you some equipment as well."

"Thanks, Slick."

"It will be waiting for you when you arrive in Berlin."

Signing off, I went in search of Manuela. I found her in the carrier's gym, dressed in blue leggings and a crop top, working through several reps of weight training. I watched as she went through a pull-down routine, her abs crunching in an impressive display.

"Like what you see?" she asked, noticing her audience and releasing the weight.

"I've seen it before," I replied. "And it's still superb."

Standing up, she ran a towel over her face and neck, then walked toward me. Leaning in close, she suggested, "Maybe you would like to get another closer look?"

"Didn't you hear," I said with a wry smile.

"What?"

"No fraternization on the carrier."

She reached out and touched my chest. "There will not be any fraternization, I promise you that."

"We'll worry about that later," I said. "Right now, I have a question for you."

"I'm listening."

"I'm heading to Minsk to find Morozov. First, I need to stop over in Berlin to collect some equipment. It will be a dangerous mission. But I'm going to need some backup."

"Okay, I'll go."

"Are you sure?"

"Yes, of course."

"Okay, will be good to have each other's back."

She smiled at me. "Speaking of backs, I need a shower. Care to help wash mine?"

"Well—"

She made a motion as though stricken with worry. "One more time, before we both die in the service of our countries."

"Since you put it that way."

———

We took a shuttle from the carrier to Berlin, where we were met by MI6 officer Ian Montrose. A long-serving intelligence man, Montrose had been stationed in Berlin for a while. He'd taken over the station chief role after the demise of Michaelson.

Taking us back to the embassy, he advised us that Christine Ryan was there to meet us.

"Wait," Holland said. "You were in Berlin, Christine?"

"Yes."

"Why weren't we told of your involvement in this operation from the start? It seems that you have more than just a passing interest."

"You know I was involved in MI6 before coming into politics just recently."

"Yes, but—"

"If there is going to be a problem, I can always recuse myself and then the inquiry will remain on hold while another is appointed."

German cleared his throat. "I don't think that will be necessary."

Holland adjusted the papers on his desk. "No, no. Not necessary."

Christine Ryan nodded. "Good. Shall we continue?"

"Good to see you, Mr. Kane. You too, Miss Garza," Christine Ryan said.

"Thank you, ma'am," Manuela replied.

"So, Mr. Kane, it would seem you have kicked up another shit storm."

"Something I'm good at, ma'am."

"Not as good as your friend, it would seem. His shit storms are on a whole other level."

I couldn't help but grin. "He does have that talent."

"Okay, let's see what we have. Tell me stories, Mr. Kane."

"You know I went to Cuba via South Korea. Once there, I was helped by the CIA but was compromised. Things went south from there. In the washup, we managed to take down Julio Garcia, kidnap the scientist from the Russian embassy, get onto a freighter off the US coast, and destroy the missiles. However, we missed Morozov."

"Not a bad day's work anyway," Christine Ryan said. "Wouldn't you say?"

"More than just one day's work, but he is still out there. If we can take him alive, we have an opportunity to find out what is happening."

"We already know. They are going to invade Poland." I was shaking my head. She looked perplexed at my response. "What is the matter?"

"They're going to take Finland."

"Why would you say that?" Christine Ryan asked me.

I explained the theory, and it was her turn to shake her head. "No, everything points to Poland."

"Poland is a fake, a ruse, a decoy."

"But all of the intelligence is pointing to it."

"The intelligence is wrong," I replied.

"All of it? I truly doubt that."

"I guess we'll find out, won't we?"

"I guess so."

"Do we have all of the equipment and paperwork we require?" I asked her.

"It will be at the hangar in the morning. Is there anything else you need?"

"No, I don't think so."

"You are booked into a nearby hotel. Please don't wreck the city like you did when you were last here."

"I can't promise you that."

"You can at least try."

———

The booking was for two rooms at the hotel. We were in Manuela's when they came for me. After checking in, we'd each taken a shower and then dressed for dinner in the restaurant. I didn't feel like any fancy food that evening and was pleased to see that there was steak and fries on their menu. I also ordered a beer. Heineken. Not a bad drop. The main course was followed by dessert. Straight-up bread pudding. If you haven't tried it, you're missing out, by the way.

Manuela and I talked and tried to forget the troubles of the world, at least for a while. Having been in the field for an extended period of time since Knocker and I had gone to Syria, I was feeling the pinch and was wearing down.

"You look tired," Manuela said to me, her voice soft and caring.

"Nothing a few weeks R&R wouldn't fix," I said.

"Yet tomorrow, you are back into the breech again."

"Yes. Some things just take precedence."

The waitress returned with another two beers, and we talked more while drinking them, enjoying the feeling of relaxation, if only for a short while. Once we finished our drinks, we headed back up to our rooms. The elevator seemed to take forever ascending the five levels to our floor, and then the chime dinged, and the doors slid open.

Manuela and I exited the lift, veering left down the gray-carpeted corridor. Our footsteps muffled against the floor as we approached our respective rooms. Manuela said to me,

"Come into my room, and I'll massage some of that fatigue out of you."

I found myself saying, "I don't think—"

"I do not mean sex, John. Just something to help you relax."

"I warn you now, I'll go to sleep."

"That is all right."

A housekeeper rumbled past us with her large laundry bin. She smiled as she passed and continued along the hallway. Manuela used her card to open the door, and I followed her into the room.

The door closed quietly behind us and locked. Manuela led the way deeper into the suite, noticing a gift had been left on a bench. Pointing at it, she said, "Look, someone loves us."

Chilling nicely in a bucket of ice was a bottle of champagne. Beside it were two glasses. Looking back now, I should have known there was something wrong, but I was too tired to think straight, and I didn't care.

Manuela poured the drinks and handed me one. After the beer, it tasted good. Us finishing those glasses was all that I remembered.

———

I stirred, disoriented in the dim confines of a swaying van. The rhythmic jostling told me we were navigating Berlin's streets. My hands were tightly bound, and a suffocating hood masked my vision. The voices I could hear were gruff, unmistakably Russian, and stirred a mix of fear and fury within me. I knew exactly who had orchestrated this abduction. Grigory Igoshin's people. How the fuck did they know I was there? My mind raced, plotting my next move.

The van bounced again, then took the next right at speed. My body was aching from being in the one position, but I wasn't willing to move just yet. I needed to gather all the intel I could before they knew I was awake.

More bumps and turns. Even beneath my hood I could sense the flicker of streetlamps as we traveled beneath them. But even those grew intermittent and then stopped altogether the farther we went. As I listened, I counted four different voices.

We veered once more, the tires now crunching against a gravel road. The vibrations reverberated through the van's chassis, jolting my entire body. Each lurch felt more violent, rattling every inch of my frame.

For the duration of the trip, I contemplated whether Manuela was in the van with me and, if she was, had she chosen to remain silent like I had.

Tearing me from my thoughts, a final lurch brought the van to a halt. Having no clue where they'd taken me, I had a feeling I was about to find out. The side door opened, and I felt hands drag me roughly to the ground. Then I heard a voice say in Russian, "Get the woman."

With that news, I had to assume that Manuela was with me. Wherever that was.

The echoing noise of being dragged across a concrete floor told me we were in a warehouse or a large shed.

Picking me up, they threw me into a chair and bound me to it, removing my hood and then slapping my face until I opened my eyes. I complied quickly. The man doing the slapping had blond hair, and the wicked scar on his cheek contributed to the snarl on his face.

"You are awake, American. In time to witness your own death. But first, we need to find out what you are up to."

"That's simple," I replied. "I'm looking for Morozov to kill him."

"He is not in Berlin."

"Fine, thanks for the intel. If you don't mind, untie me and I'll go look for him elsewhere."

"You think you are funny?" the Russian asked with a sneer.

"Not something I've been accused of before."

He hit me, hard. The blow hurt, drawing blood inside my

mouth. I spat it onto the floor and smiled. "No sense of humor, Ivan?"

He snarled and hit me again. "My name is not Ivan. It's Leonid."

"Great. I like to know the names of the men I'm going to kill."

"Get the woman," Leonid growled.

While they put Manuela in a chair across from me, I worked on my bonds. You see, they used zippy ties. And not very good ones at that. When they snapped, one of the men fixing Manuela to her seat had his back to me. Rather careless, really.

Although my head was still a little fuzzy from the drug used to sedate me, I lurched forward, managing to appropriate the Russian's weapon, which had been tucked into the back of his pants. From there, I went full Knocker.

The gun was an MP-443 Grach. Straightening, I placed it against the back of the man's head and pulled the trigger. Dropping like a stone, his body smacked into the concrete floor of the shed. In the bright lights, I could see another Russian on the other side of Manuela.

The Grach centered on his surprised face, and he made a desperate move for his own gun. It was futile of course, because the bullet I had fired was already in the air. The round punched into his head, just above his nose and he died with a surprised expression on his face.

But I was already looking for the next target. That just happened to be Leonid. He had his own weapon out, but by the time he had brought it up, he had four rounds in his chest—it took that many to put him down.

He fell like a tree and hit the hard floor with a dull thud. Behind him was another Russian, which meant I didn't have to move the Grach far at all. He died the same way the others had.

That was four down. But there were more.

Bullets cut through the cool air as I threw myself sideways, the impact of the hard concrete jarring through my body. I rolled and came up, firing at the new shooter. He took two rounds to his chest and fell away.

"John, behind you!"

Manuela's warning was a hollow echo throughout the building as I rolled and turned once more. Bullets gouged sharp slivers of concrete from the floor where I had just been, sending them flying.

The Grach came up and I fired again. This time, several rounds punched into the shooter's chest and tore through his throat. One erupted from his back in a spray of blood.

He fell to the floor, and everything stopped. There was no noise, just an eerie silence after the echoes had died away.

Manuela said, "Wow, that was intense."

I walked over to her and set her free. "Are you okay?"

"Headache and a little fuzzy."

"Me too. Has to be the drugs they gave us." I turned over the body of the leader and checked his pockets, locating a cell phone.

"That might be useful," Manuela said.

"Let's find out." I found a number that looked to be the most called and tried it. A familiar voice answered. "Hello, Grigori."

"Kane?"

"It's me. Just called to say hello, and let you know I have trimmed your wages bill a bit."

"I'm going to kill you!" he thundered.

"Line up. It seems everybody wants a piece of me these days. "Are you in Minsk?" I asked. "If so, I'll come and see you."

"Come to Helsinki. I will meet you there."

"It's a date." I disconnected the call. "Helsinki. I knew that was the target."

"What now?" Manuela asked.

"We go to Finland."

———

Using the van we had arrived in, we got back to the hotel and organized our belongings. When we were about to leave, I got a call from Holly. "Turn your television on."

I picked up the remote and flicked it on. Every channel was dominated by one thing. The Russians had rolled across the Finnish frontier with mechanized and infantry divisions. Not only that, a force had crossed the Gulf of Finland and disgorged fighters in an attempt to take over the city. Then there were the sleepers. The KGB had men inside the city already. Mercenary fighters. Igoshin's men. There were numerous fires burning throughout the city, and there appeared to be dead bodies strewn in the streets.

"I see it," I said grimly.

"The Russians have control of the air so far, but NATO is scrambling."

"What about the Americans?" I asked.

"Nothing so far. I'm starting to doubt whether they will do anything without British backing."

"Well?"

"They had the election today. Pridham got in. There's been a change of government. It's being rushed through for stability. But he's saying that he will not commit British troops to another war."

The election, I'd forgotten about that. "Shit, what is Knocker doing?"

"He's working the problem."

"I'm going to Helsinki. There is only one way to stop this now," I told her.

"John, what are you going to do?"

"Kill them all. It's the only off button I can see."

"Even Lash?" she asked.

"Especially Lash."

CHAPTER 19

WE WERE PART OF A FINNISH MILITARY CONVOY HEADED TO Helsinki from the North. Manuela and I had flown to Sweden and taken a boat across to Finland along with other reporters and news people attached to a Swedish Quick Reaction Force of an armored battalion and two infantry ones. Germany was mobilizing its forces, as was France.

Once we landed, we got a vehicle and joined the Swedish convoy. It was winter and the roads were icy. Out front of the convoy were three Leopard tanks and other armored fighting vehicles.

Two Saab JAS 39 Gripen fighter bombers flew low over the column with a sonic boom as they patrolled for any Russian threats. Smoke rose skyward on the horizon as we approached a small town.

About five kilometers out, the convoy stopped. We had a radio and were listening to transmissions. From what Manuela could decipher, the Russians were attacking the town to secure a crossroads at its center. Trapped inside was a team of Utti Jaeger Regiment special forces. They were surrounded and running out of ammunition.

Somewhere up ahead of us, orders were issued, and the tanks and an infantry company moved forward. They were supported by the two fighter bombers to relieve the pressure on the trapped troops.

So we waited and listened to the sound of battle rolling across the snow-covered landscape. The columns of black smoke ahead grew in number, and after a while, the wounded started to roll back past us to be triaged behind the column.

Encountering a captain who spoke English, I learned that he'd sustained a bullet wound to his leg. Curious about the situation, I asked him, "What's going on?"

"We tried to punch through to the Finnish troops but the Russians are holding. They brought some tanks forward to meet ours and knocked out the lead element."

"Are they all soldiers or private contractors?"

"Both. Why do contractors have tanks?"

"Igoshin does."

Suddenly, two jets screamed low overhead, leaving a supersonic boom in their wake. However, they weren't alone. Hot on their tails were three Sukhoi Su-35s. I climbed out of our armored SUV and watched them disappear. "There goes the air cover."

Toward the front of the column, a violent explosion rocked the winter landscape. An orange fireball erupted skyward. "Fuck."

I opened the passenger door and grabbed Manuela. "Out, get out."

There was soon another explosion, which was followed closely by another. "What is happening?" Manuela asked.

"Missiles."

We ran as fast as we could away from the line of vehicles, trying to put distance between ourselves and them. Moments later, realization dawned that there was no outrunning them, so we threw ourselves into a hollow in the snow.

Missiles began to rain down like explosive lances. The ground beneath us shook violently under the impacts and detonations. With our arms covering our heads, it felt as though it would never end, but it was over in several minutes.

"You okay?"

Manuela climbed to her feet. "That was fucking wild."

I stood beside her, and we stared at the column, or what was left of it. Twisted and charred vehicles continued to burn. Burned and bloody bodies were littered about on the ground. Patches of white snow were blackened by the missile impacts, while the heat had turned most to slush, and a couple of craters still had flames flickering in them.

"Look," Manuela said, pointing at our SUV.

"Luck is a fortune."

We walked back to the column and surveyed the carnage. I looked around and saw a farm track running perpendicular to the road we were on. "Come on, time to go."

"Where?" Manuela asked, looking around.

"Helsinki."

"Just like that?"

"Yes."

Climbing into the SUV, I started the engine and put it in reverse. As we inched backward out of the convoy, two journalists ran over to us. One was a woman from NBC, Hatti Gibson. The other was her cameraman, Billy Dunn. "Where are you going?" Hatti asked.

"Helsinki," I replied.

"You got room for us?"

"Where are your wheels?" I asked.

"They were damaged by a strike. I don't know how we survived."

What the hell. "Fine, get your equipment and throw it in the back."

They climbed in.

"What about your gear?" Manuela asked.

"It got hit. It's fucked."

Hatti was your typical blonde, blue-eyed camera fodder reporter. Her cameraman, I found out later, was a former ground pounder who had done three tours in Afghanistan.

Reversing up to the farm track I turned our SUV onto it. It took us through to another road that headed south. Then southeast. Manuela pointed out what I already knew. "This is headed into town."

"Yeah," I said with a nod.

"Who do you all work for?" Hatti asked.

"We're freelance," I replied.

"You're keen to go into a shit storm like this," she replied.

"Nothing we're not used to."

"You in the sandbox, man?" Dunn asked.

"Some," I replied. "Been other places as well."

"Recon?" he asked.

"Yeah."

"Figured as much. My name is Billy Dunn."

"John Kane. This is Manuela."

"I'm Hatti," the reporter added.

"What unit?" I asked Dunn.

"Twenty-third Regiment."

"How long you been shooting with cameras?"

"Five years," he replied. "You?"

"About the same," I lied.

As we continued down the road, we encountered an unexpected roadblock. Beyond it, nestled in a shadowed valley, lay a town engulfed in flames. The acrid smoke billowed upward, casting a dark stain across the sky.

The roadblock was Russian. "Who are you?" one of the soldiers who manned it asked.

"Press," I replied.

"Fuck off," he snarled.

Behind me, Dunn climbed out and started taking pictures of the town from a distance. The staccato sound of gunfire reached out to us, followed by an explosion. One of the other Russians came forward, standing in Dunn's way. "Hey! No pictures. Go away."

"I want to go down there," I said.

"No, fuck off."

The guard started pushing Dunn around. Hatti called out

to him to get back in the SUV. Dunn ignored her, and the guard hit him savagely with the butt of his weapon, sending him sprawling to the ground, his camera sliding across the gravel.

I turned around. "Hey. What the fuck are you doing?"

I advanced to help Dunn, and the soldier turned his weapon on me. He kept me covered while I picked up the cameraman. Bending again to retrieve his camera, I leaned in to return it to him and said, "Just take it easy, man, I'd like to live through this day."

"You and me both."

Guiding him toward the SUV, I waited until he had resumed his seat in the back, and then I turned back to the soldiers on the roadblock. "Which way to Helsinki?"

The one I'd spoken to gave me a sarcastic grin and pointed over his shoulder. "Right through town."

I nodded. "Thanks."

I walked back to the vehicle and climbed behind the steering wheel. Starting the motor, I put it in reverse and started to back up. Manuela said, "What now?"

"How bad do you folks want to get to Helsinki?" I asked, looking in the rear vision mirror to gauge their reactions.

"Why?"

"Because I'm going through that roadblock."

"John, no," Manuela gasped.

"It's the only way to get to Helsinki."

"Fine, but don't say you weren't warned," she replied.

"How about the NBC crew?"

"Just tell me when to duck," Hatti said nervously.

"That's the spirit."

"I'm in," Dunn said.

"Good. Now lean over the back and lift that blanket."

Intrigued, Dunn did as instructed and then let out a low whistle. "Now you're talking."

He came back with a couple of FN SCARs. "Where did you get these?"

"I know someone. Just don't use them unless it's abso-
lutely necessary. Pass the other one to Manuela."

"Who are you people?" Hatti asked.

Manuela said, "I am Grom."

"And I'm MI6, kind of," I told her.

"So, you're not reporters?"

"No."

"Oh god."

"You can get out if you want," I told her.

"No, just go. If we survive this, at least it'll give me something to write about."

We would discuss that later. In the meantime, I floored
the gas pedal, and we rocketed forward.

I could hear the shouts above the roar of the engine as the
SUV plowed through the roadblock. The Russians jumped
aside and then opened fire, the bullets rattling as they
punched into the vehicle.

I directed the SUV down the road on the icy asphalt. "Is
everyone all right?" I called out.

Thankful that nobody was hurt, I focused on our next
problem: getting through the town.

———

Most surprising to me was the absence of any further
roadblocks. All the fighters seemed confined within the town
itself. As we approached the outskirts, we encountered battle
debris: a charred truck, partially destroyed buildings, and a
few lifeless bodies. The distant sound of gunfire echoed, its
source unknown.

"We should turn here," I said as I drove up to a street.
"Try and skirt the inside of the town. Hopefully it'll get us
around."

Sudden gunfire erupted from across the street, and
bullets hammered into our SUV. "Get down!" I shouted as I
pressed the gas pedal all the way to the firewall. I turned
onto the narrow street and followed it as fast as I dared. "Is

everyone all right?"

"Been better," Billy Dunn moaned.

"Oh, no, Billy," I heard Hatti gasp. "He's been shot."

"How bad?" I asked, not slowing down.

"I don't know, there is blood everywhere."

"Billy, talk to me," I called back over my shoulder.

"It's bad. Down low, may have got my liver."

Fuck. "I can't stop just yet."

"It's okay, get us the hell out of here, man."

"Hatti, keep pressure on that wound."

"What? How?"

"Use your hands," Manuela instructed. "Just press down on it."

"O-Okay."

The SUV roared along the back street between damaged houses. A wrecked vehicle, not much more than a blackened shell, blocked the way ahead. "Damn it."

Turning hard left, I took us into a narrower street. Up ahead, another damaged vehicle blocked the way. "Hold on," I called out.

I aimed the SUV at the rear end, choosing to hit that instead of the motor-laden front. There was a sickening crunch as the SUV struck, shoving the roadblock violently out of the way. Our luck held, and although our SUV sustained some damage, it wasn't bad.

I took the next right. This street was somewhat wider but was scattered with lots of debris. It had to weave the SUV through it to stay clear. Up ahead was a T-intersection. I slowed, turned left, and slammed on the brakes.

The SUV skidded to a stop. Ahead of us was a roadblock. Only this time it was manned. Without taking my eyes from the barricade, I demanded, "Hatti, pass the Scar forward."

"The what?" she asked, her voice fearful.

"The gun."

She grabbed the weapon from the cargo hold and passed it forward, leaving a wet, sticky handprint on it. Manuela took it and raised it to the window. She looked through the sights.

"What do you see?" I asked.

"Six shooters."

"Whose?"

"Hard to tell—wait." One of the men on the roadblock pointed in their direction and raised his weapon. "Mercenaries, move!"

I ripped the shift into reverse and slammed my foot on the gas pedal. The SUV shot back and around the corner. I moved the stick again and it took off forward again. This time, I turned right.

We rocketed away from the roadblock, and I started taking turns that I hoped would benefit us. Before too long, we were deep within a labyrinthine part of the town, a part that had borne the brunt of the attack. Most of the buildings were destroyed, and it wasn't pretty.

"I can't stop the bleeding," Hatti cried pitifully from the back seat.

"Don't worry," I heard Dunn say to her. "It's not your fault."

His words absolved her of any blame. I glanced at Manuela who had looked back. She returned my look and shook her head.

"Don't worry, Billy, we'll get you some help."

"I'm done, John."

"Reaper."

"What?"

"My name. My friends call me Reaper."

I heard a soft chuckle. "You're him. The legend himself."

"I wouldn't call myself that," I replied, swerving around some rubble.

"Get Hatti to safety, huh?" he said.

"I promise."

Then he died in Hatti's arms.

I heard her sob and said, "Hatti, we don't have time for that now, grieve him later. Understand?"

"Okay."

For the next ten minutes, I did my best to avoid the built-up parts of the town until we eventually reached the other side. Once more our progress came to a halt, our passage blocked by a sentry post.

To get through, I would have to run a gauntlet. A gauntlet capped by one extremely devastating piece of military hardware: a Russian T-72 Main Battle Tank.

Reversing once again, I moved the vehicle out of sight and got out. Peering around the corner, I took in our position and predicament, searching our surroundings for a solution. There was one other way: across a snow-covered paddock that looked to be flat and almost traversable.

I went back to the SUV. "Snow chains."

"What?" Manuela looked confused.

"We're going across the field."

"Are you crazy?" she blurted out. "We have no idea what's out there."

"It's the only way."

For the next few minutes, we strapped the snow chains on the tires and, once we were ready, climbed back in. I glanced over the back at Hatti, who was still nursing Dunn's head. "You ready?"

She looked at me through tear-filled eyes. "Yes."

"Then let's go."

I started the motor, and we were off again. The SUV crashed through the wooden fence and thundered out into the field. The snow was deep, but the SUV was handling the obstacle. It lurched and bounced but kept moving.

Our forward momentum didn't last for long. Sudden explosions erupted all around us, leaving blackened scars in the snow.

I dodged and weaved, trying to avoid the blasts. We almost made it too. It was that last one before the tree line that did for us. It threw the SUV into a violent roll until it came to rest against a fence post.

For a moment, I blacked out, having hit the top of my

head on the roof. Then I realized something else. I was stuck. The seat had shifted, and I was pressed hard forward.

"Manuela, are you all right?"

"I-I think so."

"Hatti?"

She moaned.

"Manuela, can you get out?"

"Yes."

"Good, help Hatti. I'll be there in a moment."

Manuela climbed out and went to the back, assisting Hatti to escape the crumpled vehicle. Meanwhile, I was trying my best to free myself and failing miserably. "Come on, fuck you."

"What's up?" Manuela asked.

"I'm stuck."

"I'll help you," she said hurriedly.

Running around to my door, she wrenched it open. We both struggled to get me free, but it was no use. Then things went from bad to worse. Gunfire erupted and bullets started singing around the wrecked SUV.

"Go," I said to her. "Take Hatti and run!"

"What about you?"

"Don't worry about me. I'll find you in Helsinki."

"John—"

"Go! Now!"

More bullets cut close, and Manuela let out a burst of Polish profanity. "Motherfucker."

She grabbed Hatti's hand and started to run to the fence. They climbed over it and disappeared into the forest.

Moments later, the Russians arrived, and they pried me free of the wreck. Things got interesting after that.

CHAPTER 20

I WASN'T SURE HOW LONG I WAS A PRISONER FOR. LATER I would find out it was for a week. They pumped me full of drugs and interrogated me instead of brutal torture. By the time they had finished, I had no idea what I had told them or what I hadn't. Their technique was rather good and more advanced than what we knew.

"*You divulged important information to the enemy?*" Holland asked.

I shrugged. "*I have no idea. For all I know, I could have told them about the Colonel's secret herbs and spices.*"

Holly said, "*Most of what was divulged to John's captors was about the operation so far. Stuff that was already known to them.*"

"*How do you know this?*" Holland snapped. "*Were you there?*"

"*They recorded everything from the interrogation. We managed to get hold of those recordings.*"

"*Where were you taken?*" Christine Ryan asked.

They took me to a place in central Helsinki. The Russians had captured three-fourths of the capital but were under intense pressure from NATO troops. NATO airpower was reclaiming the air, and troops were pushing hard from the capital. I can remember parts.

Early on, I remember seeing Morozov and Igoshin. I

think it was Igoshin's people who drugged and interrogated me.

Lash's plan with the generals was falling apart. Thanks to our intervention, we had stopped the missiles, and America had no hesitation in backing NATO. We had also discovered that Pridham was a threat. We were closing in hard, and they were getting desperate.

Meanwhile, somewhere in the city was Manuela and Hatti. I wouldn't say that I thought of them often. I was too far out of it.

Then one night, just after two, the place where I was being held erupted in chaos. I was just coming out of a drug-induced haze. The last hit they'd given me was the morning before when they'd last questioned me. Now, as it was leaving my system, I was vomiting into a bucket. The cell lights were on. I actually don't think they were ever off.

My initial thought was that the rattle I could hear was way off in distant parts of the city where some sporadic fighting continued, hard-held bastions of freedom. There were explosions and the sound of aircraft and helicopters ripping overhead.

I heard shouts and more gunshots. This time, the fighting was closer. Much closer. The crashes made my head ring from the residual headache I was suffering from the drugs.

The gunfire I could hear died off, along with the panicked shouts. The door to my cell burst open and a figure dressed in black, with a guard tucked under his arm, strode in. He took one look at me and grinned as he shot the guard in the head. "Hello, Reaper, old mate. How the fuck are you?"

Knocker had arrived.

Cramer and Ted pushed in beside him. Cramer said, "Ted, check him out before we move him."

I stared at Knocker, his outline fading then coming back into focus. "Where the fuck have you been?"

"Saving the world, old cock. Hard fucking job to do on your own."

"Manuela," I said. "She—"

"She's in London, mate. We got her and the reporter out. You're it."

I tried to stand, but Ted held me in position. "Ease up, mate, I'm not finished."

Cramer's head dipped as he listened to an incoming transmission. Once it was done, his head came back up. "All right, gentlemen, time to go. Ted, wrap it up."

I got to my feet with the help of the others. Then I felt Knocker's arm go around me. "I got you, Reaper. Let's get the fuck out of here."

"What about Igoshin and Morozov?" I asked.

"Rats deserting a sinking ship, mate," Knocker said. "Everything is closing in on them, so they bailed."

"This doesn't end while they are all still alive," I told him.

"We'll get them. You just need to be squared away first."

He was right. It was time to leave.

———

Two days later, in the new USSR, a meeting was underway. Four men sat at a table to discuss the unfolding situation. They all blamed each other but never vocalized their opinions. Instead, they needed to come up with a new plan before it all crashed to the ground.

Lash said, "We must implement Hephaestus."

"I agree," said Morozov. "It is the only way."

"I am not sure," Shatov said. "Setting off such a weapon will have incomprehensible ramifications."

"You were fine with the missiles," Morozov pointed out.

"They were different. With them in place, we could rely on the threat to see us through. Hephaestus is a different device and scenario altogether."

"We need it to stop NATO and the Americans," Lash said. "Is it ready?"

"Another week," Morozov said. "Then we can transport it to its destination."

"I need someone I can trust to take care of it," Lash said.

"I will do it," Igoshin said.

They all stared at the mercenary boss. None could believe that a selfish man like him would volunteer for such a mission. "Are you sure?"

"My people and I will see that it gets where it needs to be."

"You know what that means, Grigori?" Shatov asked.

"Of course I fucking know what it means," Igoshin snarled.

"What about Kane?" Morozov asked.

"Forget about Kane," Shatov said. "If he is true to form, he will find us."

"Yes, but this time, kill him," Lash demanded. "The man has more lives than a fucking cat."

"He will be taken care of."

"Good. All right, this meeting is over. I will bid you all good day."

The small conference broke up, the men filing out, leaving Shatov alone. His face held a grave look of concern. Releasing Hephaestus would be devastating, not just for Europe but for Russia as well. Reaching for his cell, he dialed a number he'd been supplied with. He waited for the call to be answered and said, "There is something you should know." *"That will do for today,"* Christine Ryan said, *closing the latest chapter on our war with the generals. "We will continue tomorrow and hear from Mr. Jensen about what he was up to while the Cuban affair was unfolding."*

"Wait," German said. "Before we adjourn, what is, or was, Hephaestus?"

"Hephaestus was the Greek god of fire," I informed him.

"Yes, but what has it got to do with the Russians?"

"In short, Hephaestus was a super nuke. It had the power of wiping out not just cities, but small countries."

"And the Russians had such a weapon?"

"They sure did."

"How close did they come to using it?"

"You'll get your answers before we finish, sir," Holly told him.

German sighed. "Fine, we'll reconvene tomorrow and continue with the inquiry."

Leaving the room, we walked from the building, enjoying the last few vestiges of the retiring sun. I was welcomed by a familiar face.

"How did it go?" Manuela asked me.

"Fine. Another couple of days and we should be done."

"Do you all feel like a beer?"

Looking at Knocker and Holly, I knew they would be up for it. They nodded. I said, "Sure, why not."

As we were about to leave, my cell rang. I answered it and a familiar voice said to me, "He's ready to talk."

"We'll be right there."

I disconnected the call and looked over at Manuela. "Do you have somewhere you need to be?"

She frowned. "No."

"Good, you'll love this."

———

Night had settled across the city by the time we arrived at the house, and we were greeted by Hunt and Newman. They looked askance at Manuela and I said, "She's good. How is our guest?"

"He says he wants to see you," Newman said. "He said that he's ready to talk."

"Good."

"One thing I am curious about, how the hell did you get him?"

I smiled. "If you want the answer to that, you'll have to sit in on the remaining days of the hearing."

"There is something else you need to know, Reaper," Hunt said.

"What's that?"

"You have a visitor, John," a new voice said from the shadows of the dark.

Anesha Perera stepped into the circle of light filtering out from within the house. Hunt said, "What she said."

Everyone else moved inside, leaving me there with Anesha. "How is it going?"

"We are almost there," I replied. "A couple more days and it'll be all over."

She touched my arm. In the light, her bronze skin seemed to shine, her teeth starkly white. "Then can I have you all to myself?"

I took her in my arms. "Yes, I promise."

"Shall we go and see what the man has to say?"

I kissed her before replying. "It should be interesting. The beginning of the end."

A LOOK AT BOOK FIVE:
UNITED KINGDOM OF RUSSIA

Knocker digs deep into his dark past to find the violent version of himself he stores there...

When the world teeters on the brink of chaos, only the darkest of heroes can restore order. In this gripping action-adventure, Raymond 'Knocker' Jensen faces his most dangerous mission yet, one that forces him to dig deep into his violent past.

With nuclear threats looming, Kane is on the frontlines hunting down rogue missiles, but Jensen has a more personal mission—assassinate the traitor embedded within the highest ranks of the British government. The twist? His target has just been elected as the new Prime Minister, making this operation anything but simple.

As tensions escalate, can Jensen and Kane stop a plot that threatens to reforge the USSR?

Packed with explosive action, political intrigue, and high-stakes drama, this novel will keep you on the edge of your seat.

AVAILABLE OCTOBER 2024

ABOUT THE AUTHOR

A relative newcomer to the world of writing, Brent Towns self-published his first book in 2015. Last Stand in Sanctuary took him two years to write. His first hardcover book, a Black Horse Western, was published the following year.

Since then, he has written twenty-six western stories, including some in collaboration with British western author, Ben Bridges; several action adventure novels, such as his bestselling Team Reaper series; the novelization to the 2019 movie, Bill Tilghman and the Outlaws; as well as scripted a handful of Commando Comics. Not bad for an Australian author, he thinks.

Often up until the small hours of the night, bashing away at his tortured keyboard in Queensland, Australia, Brent loves to lose himself in the world of fiction. If you're interested in sharing your thoughts in more detail, scan the QR code below! Your feedback is invaluable to him—and often helps shape his future writing endeavors.